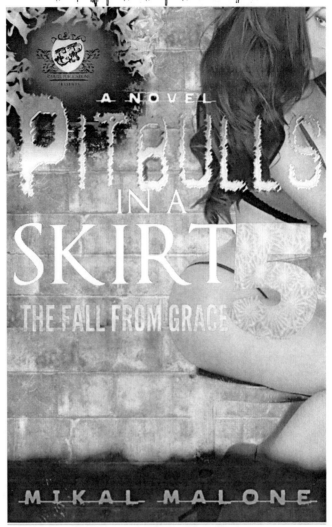

A NOVEL

PITBULLS
IN A
SKIRT 5
THE FALL FROM GRACE

MIKAL MALONE

Are You On Our Email List?

Sign Up On Our Website

www.thecartelpublications.com

Or Text The Word:

Cartelbooks To 22828

For Prizes, Contests, Etc.

M-I-K-A-L M-A-L-O-N-E

CHECK OUT OTHER TITLES BY THE CARTEL PUBLICATIONS

4

PITBULLS IN A SKIRT

WWW.THECARTELPUBLICATIONS.COM

PITBULLS IN A SKIRT 5

The Fall From Grace

By

Mikal Malone

PITBULLS IN A SKIRT

PUBLISHER'S NOTE:
This book is a work of fiction. Names, characters,
businesses,
Organizations, places, events and incidents are the
product of the
Author's imagination or are used fictionally. Any
resemblance of
Actual persons, living or dead, events, or locales
are entirely coincidental.

Library of Congress Control Number: 2016952169

ISBN 10: 0996209999

ISBN 13: 978-0996209991

Cover Design: Bookslutgirl.com

www.thecartelpublications.com
First Edition
Printed in the United States of America

What's Up Fam,

I'm not even gonna beat around the bush with a lot of talk. I'ma get straight to it! *Pitbulls in A Skirt 5: The Fall From Grace*, was nothing short of amazing! I LOVED the way T. Styles approached the latest tale in this series! Over the years, I have grown to know and love Yvette, Mercedes, Lil C and Carissa and could not wait to catch up with what's going on in their world now. I could find only one word that accurately describes this one...Vicious! But I'ma let you be the judge of it for yourself without saying too much more and possibly spoiling it for you!

Oh, if you haven't checked out *Pitbulls in A Skirt – The Movie* yet, it is Now Available in episodes on YouTube! Simply log onto YouTube and search *Pitbulls in A Skirt – The Movie* and watch all 8 episodes today!

Without further delay, keeping in line with tradition, we want to give respect to a vet or trailblazer paving the way. In this novel, we would like to recognize:

Michael Phelps

Michael Fred Phelps II is an American *former* competitive swimmer for The United States of America. He hails from the great city of Baltimore Maryland and is the most decorated Olympian of all time. He has a grand total of 28 medals, 23 of them being gold. As a HUGE fan of

swimming, I am happy to say that I have watched Michael Phelps swim his entire career in the Olympics and am extremely proud of what he contributed to the sport. We here at The Cartel Publications wish to congratulate Michael Phelps on ALL his accomplishments and wish him happiness and blessings in his retirement.

Aight, get to it. I'll catch you in the next novel.

Be Easy!

Charisse "C. Wash" Washington
Vice President
The Cartel Publications
www.thecartelpublications.com
www.facebook.com/publishercwash
Instagram: publishercwash
www.twitter.com/cartelbooks
www.facebook.com/cartelpublications
Follow us on Instagram: Cartelpublications
#CartelPublications
#UrbanFiction
#MichaelPhelps
#PrayForCeCe

MIKAL MALONE

CARTEL URBAN CINEMA'S 2nd WEB SERIES

IT'LL COST YOU – T. STYLES TWISTED TALES
EPISODE ONE AVAILABLE on YOUTUBE

August 30, 2016

www.youtube.com/user/tstyles74

www.cartelurbancinema.com

www.thecartelpublications.com

PITBULLS IN A SKIRT

CARTEL URBAN CINEMA'S 1ˢᵗ WEB SERIES

THE WORST OF US (Season One)

NOW AVAILABLE:
YOUTUBE/AMAZON STREAMING

&

DVD

www.youtube.com/user/tstyles74
www.amazon.com
www.cartelurbancinema.com
www.thecartelpublications.com

M-I-K-A-L M-A-L-O-N-E

CARTEL URBAN CINEMA'S 1st MOVIE

PITBULLS IN A SKIRT – THE MOVIE
Now Available

www.cartelurbancinema.com,
www.youtube.com/tstyles74
and
www.amazon.com
www.thecartelpublications.com

#PitbullsinASkirt5

MIKAL MALONE

ACKNOWLEDGEMENTS

I'd like to thank all Pitbulls In A Skirt fans who enjoy these characters as much as I do. A book is nothing without readers to share it with. It means more to me than you know.

Mikal Malone aka T. Styles

Email: authortstyles@me.com

www.facebook.com/authortstyles or T. Styles *Fan Page*

www.twitter.com/authortstyles

DEDICATION

This book is dedicated to Cartel Publications fans

everywhere.

We love you!

PITBULLS IN A SKIRT

PROLOGUE

PRESENT DAY

A blanket of thick snow covered Washington DC coating Marjorie Gardens, a drug induced project within the city, ran by the Pitbulls with Lil C at the helm. Over 28 inches of snow deadlocked the city like falling concrete making it impossible for a single car to pass on the roads, including the police.

All was silent.

Eerily silent.

Until a hail of gunfire crashed into the apartment doors on the seventh floor inside one of the massive brick colored buildings. Making things appear as if a war had taken place on US soil.

The predators?

Many.

The prey?

PITBULLS IN A SKIRT

Mercedes, Yvette and Carissa. As well as the kilos of cocaine they had nestled inside apartment #745.

Feeling responsible for it all, Yvette looked at her warped reflection through the closed steel elevator door, Mercedes' bloodied body barely hung at her side. Just that one day alone Yvette had experienced more bloodshed then she had in over a year, during the Black Water Klan Massacre. And yet her heart told her there was more bloodshed and despair to come her way.

Her major fear was that the Grim Reaper would knock soon and claim another of her friends and to prevent this fate she was prepared to give her life.

And the way the bullets were popping off, she may have to.

CHAPTER ONE

YVETTE

FIVE HOURS EARLIER

"We ran DC!"

I could barely hear my friends' voices as they stood in front of me as I sat on the sofa; while they yelled hate filled words at each other.

Periodically I would glance down at my diamond bezel watch to check the time, secretly questioning when they would ever stop.

We drank too much to pass the time lately and I wondered if the years of moving dope had finally turned against our bodies and minds. Being hunted all of your life can do that.

Still, I tried to count my coke blessings.

After a few setbacks we were back on top!

Well...kinda.

PITBULLS IN A SKIRT

At one point we were living in Toi's basement and the next we were put back on in a major way, thanks to Bambi Kennedy of the Pretty Kings helping us out with the Black Water Klan whose only mission in life was to hunt us down and kill us. With the firepower the Pretty Kings possess they were able to murder most of the Klan with the exception of Karen and Oscar who are still out there probably plotting our demise.

Safety wasn't a problem. With the exception of today we keep security surrounding us at all times so I'm not worried about that bitch but it doesn't mean my eyes don't remain open.

With the way my friends were cutting each other down verbally I wondered if we hadn't finally become our own worst enemy and would do the work for Karen and her son.

What shocked me was not that we drank a little more than usual but that my friends didn't seem to be happy that we're finally bosses again.

I hated being broke but they acted the same no matter what.

Normally we'd have a beer along with a few tequila shots but tonight we drank and drank and drank until only a little liquid rested at the bottom of

the bottles. Whenever that happened thoughts of the past and everyone we lost resurfaced for me.

But for Carissa and Mercedes things turned much darker.

It was as if they hated one another.

"Bitch, he don't fuck with you," Mercedes yelled to Carissa as they stood in front of me. She took her long shoulder length hair and tied it into a bun on the top of her head that rolled slightly to the left. "So why is that my fault again?" The sun shining through the balcony caressed the diamond cross that hung at the introduction of her cleavage.

"You and Lil C do all you can to stop Ryan from liking me," Carissa responded, her silky black hair in a single braid that ran down her back. Her weight even more gaunt than it had been in the past. "It's not fair."

I rubbed my throbbing temples and ran my hand through my short black hair. I was trying not to allow their negative energy to spill over me but it was difficult whenever they were like this. We weren't even supposed to be in Marjorie let alone in our plush apartment this long.

We had beautiful homes off the property complete with servants.

Our coke was dropped off here instead of our regular spot because of the snowstorm that had come our way. At first we thought about delaying the shipment until the snow died down but I didn't trust it. Not accepting the package meant it would be held up at a location we wouldn't have access to for weeks, causing the streets to run dry when the weather cleared up.

I couldn't have that.

We needed to be near our keys at all times.

We ran DC!

And since I don't like my money fucked with I suggested a coin flip to see who would have to get snowed in with the dope in Marjorie. But Carissa and Mercedes refused, claiming to always come in on the losing in of a flip. Their turndown of my offer meant all three of us would have to stay, since Lil C was out of town on drug business.

"Can ya'll stop this shit already?" I begged. "I'm sick of going through this every other night. You bitches act like he's a dog or something. Ryan is a child and both of your blood."

They both looked down at me. "Stay out of it, Vette." Carissa pointed at me. "This 'tween me and this whore."

Mercedes moved closer to Carissa, a hard frown etched across her face. "One more time, Carissa." She placed her hands together as if she was praying. "I'm begging you to call me out my name one more time and watch if I don't smack the lashes off your face."

Carissa laughed and waved her hand so close to Mercedes' that I thought she rubbed her nose. "You wish you were that bold." Her posture suddenly stiffened.

Mercedes moved even closer. "You heard what I said. Just one more time and see what'll happen."

Carissa smiled and I knew this was not about to end well. "Fuck...you...WHORE."

PITBULLS IN A SKIRT

At first all I saw was the white of Mercedes' palm. Then came her hand on Carissa's face so quick if you blinked you might have missed it. Carissa's brown skin quickly reddened under the blow. Mercedes slapped her so severe she fell to the floor causing Ryan, their five-year-old grandchild to wake up when he heard the thump.

You'd think Lil C and Persia having a baby together would bring them closer but it was far from the case. Low key Carissa blamed Mercedes for forcing her to choose between her daughter's life and Lil C's, the night Karen and Oscar from the Black Water Clan kidnapped them both.

They were all about to be killed.

But in the end, using the doctrine that the Black Water Klan followed Carissa was able to negotiate Lil C and her grandson Ryan's life, which meant Persia ultimately had to die. The ordeal was so brutal Karen cut the baby out of Persia's gut leaving Carissa traumatized forever. Persia had chosen the Klan over her family anyway so in my opinion it made sense but I had never been a mother either.

"I'm gonna kill you, bitch," Carissa yelled as she charged Mercedes. Her eyes cold as the snow.

The fight had officially begun.

I watched as two grown women, worth millions, rolled around on the carpet of this three-bedroom apartment. If someone looked inside from the window they would think they were on drugs, not bosses responsible for over a million dollars worth of cocaine in apartment #745.

I watched them for a second but when Carissa's big toe tapped my chin I had enough. I leapt up, grabbed the .45 tucked in the cushion and cocked it, pointing the barrel at the ceiling. Since we were all conditioned to the sound of a gun loading they froze in place and gazed at me as if I was the crazy one.

"It's two feet of snow outside and climbing!" I smirked at them. "None of us want to be here but we don't have a choice. Now if I gotta be snowed in with ya'll fighting I'd rather kill both you bitches and be by myself. So what you wanna do?"

Carissa used the couch to stand on her feet. Dusting her dark blue True Religion Jeans off at the knees she took a deep breath. "As irritated as I am you can pull the fucking trigger." Carissa said. "I'm sick of both of you bitches anyway."

She flopped down on the sofa and picked up Ryan who cried harder when he was in her arms. It wasn't until Mercedes walked over and removed him from her that he settled down and went back to sleep. Noticing how Mercedes seemed to seduce their grandchild caused Carissa to grow angrier.

"You see that shit, Yvette?" She frowned pointing at Mercedes and Ryan. "And ya'll want me to think she not sabotaging our relationship. Get the fuck out of here."

Mercedes laughed. "You so jealous."

"How am I jealous? Because you turning my grandson against me?"

"I would never do something so stupid," Mercedes yelled pointing at her.

"Then how come it don't like me?"

"Maybe because you keep calling Ryan an 'IT'. He has a name, maybe you should use it some times."

The more they argued over dumb shit the angrier I grew. "I'm so sick of this." I tucked the gun into my designer jeans. "We family and you'd think after losing Kenyetta we would be better for it. And closer."

"I don't know why you sick of it, if you ask me this all your fault," Carissa said to me.

I frowned. "How you figure?"

"We have beautiful homes in the suburbs. But because you had one of the largest shipments delivered this year we have to be snowed in together here. We don't even hang out anymore. Now we're forced to

spend hours together on some business shit? Of course we want to kill each other." She paused. "And only God knows what Treasure and Chante doing at my house right now."

"First off I never told you to let Treasure and Chante stay in the house while we accepted the delivery. You had Melinda's number and could've called her to watch them. Plus it's not like they aren't old enough to look out for each other anyway."

"Stop fucking complaining, Carissa," Mercedes said. "That's all you do is complain."

"Complaining?" Carissa said with her jaw hung. "We have over 30 kilos of cocaine in this building. If the FEDS planned a raid after they plow we locked up for life."

"I know that!" I yelled. "Why you think I had it posted up at another spot in the building instead of here?" I asked. "I'm not dumb."

"Like that's gonna work. If the FEDS come who you think they gonna believe the weight belongs to?" Carissa continued. "Quentin and Kliyo young asses or the three kingpins on the 8th floor who they been watching for years?"

"Then what you want me to do? Lil C getting held up at the airport and the snowstorm meant we had to be here."

"Let's keep it basic because I know what this is really about," Carissa said to me. "And why you so calm and unconcerned."

I frowned. "And what's that?"

"As long as you got Heavy you good with being here. I wouldn't be surprised if things hit the fan, you chose him over us too."

"Yeah, Carissa talking some real shit now," Mercedes added. "Because of this shit I can't see Jackson until they dig us out. Which may be forever."

I laughed sarcastically. "I'm not about to argue with either of you about the decision we made together. We're here now so we can either deal with it or not. I wasn't mad at first but the way I'm feeling right now I wouldn't care if either of you bitches killed yourselves." I stormed off.

CHAPTER TWO

GRACE

"I'm begging you not to leave me. But if
I can't stop you, I'll stop her."

*T*he *open windows cooled down the tiny bedroom as
Grace Johnson did her best to fight for her
relationship.*

Sadly it wasn't working.

*"Can you at least tell me again why you're breaking up
with me?" Grace pleaded as she watched Heavy pack his
clothing in a rushed fashion. Her light brown box braids
hung over her shoulders and clung to her skin due to her
sweating so much. "You act like you don't even know me."*

*"Why you keep asking the same shit?" Heavy tossed a
white t-shirt over his right shoulder. He was placing his
neatly folded clothing into a black leather duffle bag
preparing to make his escape from her. Standing 6'3 he was a*

big dude with a facial expression that would scare those who didn't know him. "This ain't no game." His nostrils opened and closed with each breath. "Start recording the shit I say to you, maybe then you'll remember."

Grace paced the floor a few times, clutched her hands in front of her and took a deep breath. "I'm not trying to make you upset. All I want to know is if you still love me?"

"Grace, if you think what you see in my eyes right now is love then you still on them pills." He paused. "I don't love you anymore and you already know it."

"Heavy, we – "

"You think I don't know what you doing tonight?" He yelled, causing her to blink with each word. "You think I don't know you came over during the snow storm hoping to get snowed in with me, so you could fuck shit up with my shawty? You not smarter than me, Grace. Never have been and never will be."

Her lips tightened and her expression was weighty with guilt. "That's not true. I came over to get the rest of my clothes."

He laughed. "You mean those two hooker dresses you have in my closet?" He rushed over to it, grabbed a red dress *and a tiger striped one off hangers and threw them in her face.*

"You didn't have to do that!" She tossed them to the floor. "Anyway I came for Megan's stuff too. My mother wants them."

"For what? Her fat ass can't even fit into the clothes she wearing now so what she gonna do with children's clothing?" He took a deep breath. "Our daughter is dead. Remember? You left that window open and she fell out eight months ago." He pointed over her right shoulder, his forearm brushing against the side of her face.

Although he was angry her pussy tingled because it was the first time he touched her since the funeral. And he only laid hands on her that moment with a hug, doing his best to erase some of the grief from losing their child. Even before their daughter's death they hadn't been sexual with each other in five months prior because he was done with her conniving ways.

Her name may have meant goodwill but she was anything but. If the truth glistened the more she didn't get her way after asking the deadlier she got.

They both knew it.

Grace would never give him up without a fight. Eugene 'Heavy' Carter was the only man she'd ever loved in her 25-year-old life. Losing him didn't only mean her relationship was over, it meant the end of the world, as she knew it. She wouldn't call it quits until she pulled every dirty trick from her bag the streets taught her.

"You must feel real strong, standing in front of me and telling me I'm responsible for killing my own child. You have no emotions at all for me do you?"

"You did kill her, Grace. You and I both know it and because of it I will never forgive you."

She stumbled backward against the open window like a boxer coming in on the losing in of a punch in a title bout. "That's not true! I said stop saying that to me!"

He shook his head. "Deliberately or not, had you been watching her my only child would be alive today." He zippered the duffle and lifted it off the bed. "Like I said...I don't love you no more, Grace. And I'm not about to fuck up my new relationship because you can't get that through your brain."

"It's because of her money isn't it?"

"Grace – "

"I won't let her have you." Her forehead crinkled causing her to look twice her young age. *"I won't let you walk around Marjorie, knowing you belonged to me. Making people laugh at me or worse, feel sorry for me."* She stepped closer, her breasts brushing at his abdomen because he was so tall. *"But if you choose to go that route I will wreak more havoc than you can imagine, Heavy. Even more than you think I am capable of. When it comes down to it, you really don't know me."*

"Are you threatening me?" He asked while squaring his large frame directly in front of her and peering down into her eyes.

"No...I'm begging you not to leave me. But if I can't stop you, I'll stop her." She exhaled, looked down at her hands and back up at him. He was so gigantic it seemed as if her eyes would never reach his but when they did she frowned. *"When you were last inside of my pussy you said I belonged to you. And I took those words very seriously."*

Heavy took a deep breath and tried to compose himself. It wasn't because he was fearful. One swipe of his hand and he could have her in the hospital for weeks. Body to body she was no match for him but he underestimated the stamina of a woman in love and obsessed.

"It's over. I don't know another language to say it in. Let yourself out." He looked at her once more and walked around her.

But Grace didn't leave the building. Instead she stood in their old bedroom and tried desperately to inhale the scent of his expensive cologne. She had to resort to those types of things in order to grasp any reminders of how things use to be when they were together.

When they were in love.

When his scent faded away, finally she stumbled through the door and into the living room where her friends Rambler and Kitty were sitting on the sofa waiting for the verdict.

Did she win him back or nah?

Was there hope for them, who also had been dumped by their dudes?

When Grace first extended the invitation to her friends it seemed like a great idea. She would bring them along in the event that Yvette, Mercedes and Carissa were in the apartment. She figured together the six of them would fight but things didn't go as planned and now their presence acted as an additional reminder that Heavy was gone.

Possibly forever.

PITBULLS IN A SKIRT

*"So it didn't work?" Rambler asked sliding the red
Chicago Bulls cap further down over her bleached blonde
curly hair. "So you telling me we got stuck over here for
nothing? Without a nigga or dick?"*

*Kitty scratched her thick brown thigh and leaned back.
"Mannnn, I was looking forward to stomping some drug
boss asses." She cracked her knuckles for effect even though
they hurt.*

*Grace's shoulders hunched forward. She was short,
standing 5'4 and that's if you gave her credit for her thick
soled sneakers. But she was also the loudest, the strongest
and the most deadly of her friends. Which was why they
hated seeing her in such dire straits.*

*"He really leaving me," Grace said trying not to have a
hard cry. "He blaming me for our daughter and everything."*

*Rambler and Kitty looked at one another and shook their
heads.*

"That fat bastard," Rambler said.

"Easy," Grace warned. "He's still my nigga."

"Well what you wanna do about that?" Kitty asked.

*"Because I know one thing...we can't let him get away
with treating you like this." Rambler, who was always ready
for drama said. "And you know I can't stand them bitches*

anyway. They think just cause they got money they better than the rest of us in Marjorie."

Grace nodded in acknowledgment and looked around the brown torn carpet hoping to come up with an idea worthy of her heavy heart.

"I don't know the major plan but might I suggest getting high in the mean time?" Kitty asked. "I brought some smoke."

"Bitch, don't be stupid," Rambler said. "We dealing with something else right now. Grace might have lost her nigga for good."

They both looked at her, hoping she'd given them the slightest direction no matter how dangerous. "Yvette took something from me...so let's take something from her. I'll start with her peace of mind."

"Sounds like it's about to be one crazy night," Rambler grinned. "Let's get to it."

CHAPTER THREE

MERCEDES

"You should've asked before you sent two niggas over my house!"

From where I sat I could still see the snow falling from the sky, in a heavy powder that was doing its best to keep us here even longer. "I'm fine," I said to Lil C as I sat on the sofa sipping a cup of hot ginger tea. We were talking on the phone. "You act like I'm a newbie at this and I wish you'd stop worrying."

He sighed. "I know you 'bout the game, ma but you weak right now. The worst thing that could've happened was the window break in Marjorie. We haven't run shit forever there. It's not like Emerald City." Window Break was code word for early dope delivery.

"But nobody knows about the window break."

"Niggas ain't stupid, ma. All three of the bosses are in Marjorie at the same time? Come on now. Even if

39

they not sure they gonna try their hands, especially with me being out of town. And it won't make no never mind that ya'll are bosses either, ma." He paused. "Not only that, but Kliyo and Quentin never been responsible for this much work. Don't get me wrong, up until this point they been good but money has a tendency to show you what's really pumping through a nigga's veins. Loyalty or greed. "And I don't—"

"Lil C—"

"Cameron, ma." He interrupted. "I'm not Lil C no more I keep telling you that. And I know you never got over the beef with dad but I appreciate being called by my given name. I had to punch a nigga in the mouth the other day for calling me Lil C, thinking the shit was comical because you keep saying it 'round the way."

I sighed because he was right. He definitely had grown up over the years still, it's hard not to call him by the name that reminded myself and even him that his father, the only man I loved deeply, was gone.

By my hands at that.

"You right...Cameron. But I'm fine at Marjorie."

"And since I got everything to do with it you gonna stay that way too," he said. "So how's your grandson?"

I frowned. "Wait, you calling me as if I wouldn't give up breath and life for this little boy?" I held on to the diamond cross on my neck, caressing my thumb over it.

"What part of my words got you coming at me that way?" He paused. "I was just asking how my son was that's all. Don't be mad at me because I checked you on that Lil C shit."

I laughed. "I'm not tripping off of that," I lied. "I just wanted to remind you that I'm still the woman who raised you and Chante alone. That means Ryan is always good with me."

"But dad was around too. May not have been in the way you wanted but he was always there. I know niggas that couldn't recognize their pops' face if they stole them. I remember mine."

"As long as you don't forget who was full time in your life. Because it wasn't your *Dad* that's for sure."

He exhaled. "I ain't call you to argue, or weigh who was the best parent. I just wanted you to know that I'm not a fan of my mother being snowed in with that thing." He paused, talking about the drug shipment. "But I love you all the same."

Expecting him to come at me another way I was caught off guard. Suddenly all of the tension I felt was released like air from a balloon being poked by a pin. "That was sweet."

"That was true," he said seriously. "I might give these birds a hard time out here but when it comes to you I'm solid. You'll forever have my heart, ma."

I smiled. "I love you too, son."

"Good, so you can understand what I'm about to do next."

Click.

I frowned. "Cameron?" I looked at my cell phone but it was obvious he was gone. "Lil C! Where you go?" I called his name several times but received no answer. It was obvious he hung up leaving me with many unanswered questions.

What had he done?

And more than it all, how would it impact me?

PITBULLS IN A SKIRT

I watched as Heavy stood in front of a black cast iron pan full of hot frying chicken. Yvette was at his side and was seasoning a second batch. I was happy for her to have the type of love that I wanted with Jackson even if I was skeptical if their new bond was real.

And as far as me, my heart was somewhere else at the time.

Anyway, Jackson and Heavy were two different men.

Jackson was more easy going, wanting nothing more than to be the perfect man for me, whatever that meant. Heavy's personality was darker and he was more controlling. Now that I think about it I wonder if we didn't gravitate to the same kind of men who first broke our hearts...Cameron and Thick.

Considering how we ended up killing them both I can't help but wonder if fate wouldn't deal us similar hands.

Could we murder our men again if necessary?

Don't even get me started with Derrick.

It's amazing after all of these years Yvette was mostly the same with the exception of one thing. She got prettier. Along with the money she earned and the power she possessed, she quickly became one of the most wanted women in Marjorie Gardens, just like she had in Emerald.

We were all desired but she got far more looks than she realized.

Still a shorty with big titties and a round ass her baby phat faded away and introduced her curves. I smiled as the light from the open window kissed her smooth amber complexion. And the scar she created when she used a knife to slice across her face, moments before killing Thick.

At 5'5 inches, she was still the meanest bitch you could ever come across. And I got the impression she could do the dope gave forever.

Wish I could say the same.

PITBULLS IN A SKIRT

I was just about to steal a wing when there was a knock at the front door. Yvette and Heavy turned around to look at me as Carissa crawled out of the bedroom door to go answer it with an attitude as usual. Looking out the peephole she asked, "Who is it?"

"Fresh," a deep voice I recognized called out from the other side. "And 88."

Carissa looked at me and frowned. "Why they here?"

I exhaled and shook my head. Lil C overstepped majorly. "I know why...open the door." I crossed my arms over my chest.

"Bitch, before I do that tell me why they here," Carissa continued. "We have to be careful around here."

I took a deep breath. "Lil C sent them."

"Lil C, I mean Cameron, what are you doing sending them here?" I asked in a hushed tone as I stood in the corner. I was talking to him on the phone. From where I was posted I saw the expression on Yvette and Carissa's faces and neither of them appreciated the new security. We didn't like people watching over us this way. "I am a grown woman and you should've asked before you sent two niggas over my house."

"It ain't your house, although its fly, it's just an apartment ya'll have to crash at in the Gardens. You live in the burbs remember?" He paused. "That's what I'm saying...you been there too long and I need somebody to keep eyes on you and my aunts while I'm not there. So they not moving."

"Cameron, I'm serious! I'm not a child."

"Ma, it's not about that. You think I sent them niggas to watch ya'll because I don't think you an adult? I sent them because you my mother and ya'll being snowed in with no way out got me feeling uncomfortable. I'm not there to protect you so I sent two dudes I know are loyal to me from Marjorie."

"But, Cam—"

"Ma, I love you and I mean no disrespect but they staying." He sighed. "And I gotta go. I'm trying to see when the next flight gonna take off so I can be on it and back to DC, but it don't look good. I'll talk to you soon."

Dropping my cell in my pocket I looked up at the ceiling sighed and walked over to my friends and C's squad. "Talk to C?" 88 asked me. "Did he clear up everything?"

88 stood 6'3 and had skin the color of coffee with a little extra cream. His hair was cut low and he brought with him a powerful presence whenever he walked into the room. Fresh on the other hand was a big dude who always smelled good and was a favorite among the ladies in Marjorie for his flirtatious ways.

I placed one hand on my hip and the other on my forehead. "Yeah," I said to 88. "I talked to him and he told me why you came."

"We don't mean to cause any problems," Fresh said. "We'll stay near the door and out the way if ya'll want us to. It's just that Cameron sounded pretty serious about us staying to make sure things go smooth tonight."

"Yeah, both of you can stand next to the door because I'm not feeling this shit one bit," Carissa said placing her hands on her hips. "Lil C exceeded all boundaries this time, Mercedes." She pointed at me. "And some how I'm not surprised because you're his fucking mother. You better keep him in line." She rolled her eyes and stormed into the back.

88 grabbed two chairs from around the dining room table and dragged them by the door. "We'll post right here to stay out the way. It's not a prob—"

"Nonsense," Yvette said waiving her hand. "No I don't feel like being babysat but I also know that if Lil C's doing it it's because he cares about us. And I'm not about to have the men he sent being treated like shit." She took a deep breath. "Personally I doubt anybody will be crazy enough to fuck with us tonight but since you're both here I might as well feed you."

"Thank you, Yvette," 88 said looking at me and back at her. "I 'ppreciate it. Haven't had anything all day."

Yvette and me walked toward the kitchen, with Heavy and our new security hovering behind us.

CHAPTER FOUR

KLIYO AND QUINTON

"We locked in without pussy. That's
when it becomes a problem for me."

T *he window was open as Kliyo and Quinton sat at the
kitchen table with a deck of playing cards in front of
them, kilos of coke to the left in huge bags labeled dog food.
"You gonna cheat all night, nigga?" Quinton asked as he
lifted his black fitted Redskins cap to scratch his head.
"Because I'm about to throw my hand in if that's the case."*

*Kliyo frowned. "Nigga, stop acting like a bitch. Ain't
nobody cheating on your — "*

*When 'The Phone' rang Kliyo pushed the cards off the
table and hurriedly answered, knowing it could be only one
person since no one else had the number. "Hey, 'Vette."*

*"Hey, shit, nigga, you watching that work right?"
Yvette asked digging into his ass for points.*

*"Uh...yeah...we...um," he kicked the cards behind him.
"We just waiting on relief that's all. But you can count on*

us, Yvette. No worries on this end." He scratched in between the rows of his braids.

"Listen, relief is coming soon. So don't worry about all that. I just need you to keep your eyes peeled in the meantime," she paused. "And don't let nobody in that apartment. Not your mama, your son or your bitch."

"Vette, you know I wouldn't do that. I'm not crazy." He smiled as if she could see him. "Trust me, everything will remain untouched when you get here."

Quinton rolled his eyes witnessing how nervous he was.

"That goes for Quinton too," Yvette continued. "You been doing good around Marjorie which is why we picked you. If this night goes without a hitch you gonna be doing better."

"It's gonna be a quiet ass night on this end."

"Yeah, aight, nigga."

When he ended the call Quentin chuckled. "You know she couldn't see the cards right?" he said shaking his head. "I know she the Plug but she ain't got X-Ray vision, nigga."

Kliyo picked the cards up from the floor and slammed them on the table. He leaned back and exhaled finally being able to breathe. Dealing with Yvette was always so intense for him and if the truth was heard he was the fuck scared of her. *He saw the things she did to niggas who dabbled with her money or her product and he didn't want to be anywhere near her 'Don't Fuck With You' side.*

"I know, but that bitch be wildin', man. I heard she cut off a nigga's dick one time when the money was short." He ran his hand down his clammy face. "Those kinds of stories fuck with a nigga's head for life. You gotta be careful with her." He knocked his temples with his knuckles.

Quinton stood up and walked to the fridge and removed one beer for himself. "You know relief not coming right?"

Kliyo's eyes widened. "But she said they were coming once − "

"Have you looked outside, man?" He pointed to the window. "Ain't nobody coming out this bitch no time soon. The snow touching niggas kneecaps. We in here two days tops and that's if I'm being generous. Could even take a week since you know the government digs the niggas out last." He sighed. "I don't mind with the pay they give but we locked in without pussy. That's when it becomes a problem for me." He gulped all of his beer and tossed the can in the trash.

Kliyo sighed. "I know...and Lay-Lay wanted to stop by earlier and bring her friend too." Kliyo shook his head. "If I knew all this I would've said yes."

Quinton rushed up to him and gave him the stare of death. "You mean to tell me we could've had In-Trap Pussy and you refused it?" He slapped him in the back of his head. "What you need...medication or somethin'?"

Kliyo rubbed his throbbing scalp. "Nah, man, 'Vette said we not supposed to have bitches in the trap. I'm not trying to chance that shit."

Quinton laughed hard and for what seemed like an eternity. "Are you that scared of that bitch that you caught a fever?" He pointed at the door. "Ain't nobody coming in here. That's what I'm trying to tell you."

"Nah...I..."

"Do you know why they got us sitting with a package worth over a million?" He asked looking at the Dog Food bags.

Kliyo's brows lowered. "You know it's worth a million?"

"Nah...I'm guessing but I know it wasn't supposed to stop here. Since when have we ever gotten a re-up this large? This storm fucked up their plan, trust me. It wasn't supposed to come here."

Kliyo scratched his scalp. "I thought they got us sitting with it because we always hold the package."

"Nah, man. A drop this big gotta be distributed to the city. Not just Marjorie. And they got us sitting with it because if the FEDS did a surprise run through, they don't want to be nowhere near it. Instead they electing to micromanage by being in the building and shit."

"But if a regular car can't get in how the FEDS gonna make it?" Kliyo asked.

"I don't know all that." He shrugged. "They probably think cameras set up in the building or something. Drug bosses have a tendency to be noid. Listen, do you remember when they banged that Spanish-Jamaican cat out New York? The FEDS found out he was getting a package during the storm and figured he would be snowed in with his work so nobody could fuck with it. Instead of going by land the FEDS went by air, and gave him life with no parole when they caught him with all them keys. Last I heard he hadn't seen his mother's eyes in ten years."

"So what, nigga?"

"So, them bitches have no intentions on coming down here, Kliyo. We can have who ever we want in the spot and they'll never be the wiser. As long as the whores not making excessive noise we good."

Kliyo thought about his conniving words and already his dick was thumping. "It sounds good but I don't know about this, man. I got a feeling this move can go a million wrong ways."

"Well I do know about it." He sighed. "No offense, you my man and all, but I'm not trying to get locked in with a dusty ass nigga with funky feet for two days. If I can get me some Slide In that's what I want." He grabbed his dick.

Kliyo frowned. "My feet don't stink."

"You know what I mean."

Kliyo stood up. "Even if I did sanction your plan where we gonna get two broads from now? Lay-Lay got walled in with some nigga out Virginia. He snatched her before the snow came down good, right after I said no."

"Fuck!" Quinton said boxing the air. "If I knew somebody else in this building I would put a call in. I wouldn't even care how they face look if they pussy —"

There was a knock and both men grabbed their gats before cocking them and aiming in the direction of the door. Slowly Kliyo moved toward the door and looked out the peephole. When he got a good view he turned around and leaned up against the door in total shock.

"You won't believe this shit," Kliyo whispered.

"Who the fuck is it?" Quinton asked, weapon still trained on the door.

"Two bitches. I couldn't see their faces. All I saw was titties in tight dresses."

Quinton frowned. "What man? You sound crazy."

"Titties...that's all I saw."

Quinton rushed him, pushed him to the side, looked out the peephole and smiled. "I don't want to be presumptuous but I think Christmas came early for two niggas in the city."

"Why you say that?"

"It's sexy ass Grace and Rambler." He gripped his crotch. "It don't get no better than this nigga! We fucking tonight!" He unlocked and removed the security bar that was across the door to open it and smiled at the tight dresses they wore.

Rambler was dipped in a red dress that cut low on her breasts while Grace sported an even shorter tiger stripe one. They were summer outfits that she left over Heavy's after she moved out because they didn't fit her anymore.

Certainly too much for the storm but perfect for her plan.

The whorish gear certainly came in handy.

Holding a red ceramic mug Grace grinned and liked her lips "Got sugar?"

Kliyo opened the door wider. "How 'bout you come in here and find out."

Grace and Rambler fucked Quinton and Kliyo side by side on the living room floor. Flat on her back, legs spread open Rambler was surprised at how well Kliyo stroked her inner walls. Had she known being with him would've been so good she would've got with him a long time ago. As a matter of fact if things worked out she had plans on fucking him again at the bottom of the week. Especially since her dude let her go earlier.

Grace on the other hand was on some other shit.

This was all business.

PITBULLS IN A SKIRT

On all fours as Quinton dug into her pussy from behind she looked around the apartment taking in everything. All she saw was large bags of dog food, but where was the animal?

She grinned when she realized that was the pack.

She knew about the Trap because she overheard Kliyo bragging to someone that he finally got with the Pitbulls and was clocking in big bucks. After a few calls to people in the building she got exactly what she wanted, the apartment number and access.

The plan was to get inside, call Heavy and offer him an ultimatum. Either come back to her, or she would make him a part of her devious plans.

CHAPTER FIVE

ROCKY

MOMENTS EARLIER

"It's not our business now but it can be."

R ocky looked out the peephole in the apartment she shared with her friends, on the same hallway but to the left of The Trap, the far opposite end of the elevator. After seeing Grace and Rambler walk inside with freak dresses on she turned around and gave her predictions to her friends. "Five to one Mercedes and them don't know them bitches in the Trap."

She leaned against the door and wiped her straight fire red died hair from her light face.

White Girl Kisha shrugged as she munched on a big bag of cheese Doritos. Her hair in two long French braids that hung down her back. "Girl, please. For all you know they may work for them."

"Or maybe it's empty," Dukes who sat at the glass table in the kitchen playing solitaire said. Her natural hair in two thick puffs on top of her head. "You never know."

"The Trap is never empty," Rocky advised taking one last look out the peephole before flopping on the sofa next to Kisha. She was bored out of her mind and looking for some trouble disguised as adventure. "It might not be fully loaded with dope but I bet money inside. I think we on to something big."

"Can I have your chips?" Kisha asked Rocky as she rubbed her pregnant belly, not even five months aged. "Little Crank eating his face off in here."

Rocky rolled her eyes and slapped the back of her hand on her other palm. "Before we got snowed in I specifically said to get your own liquor, snacks and necessities. And what you do? Go to the store, get ice cream and eat it all up in two hours. Forgetting we gonna be here for days. Now you want my shit too? Nah…"

Kisha huffed and rolled her eyes. "Whatever…"

Dukes laughed. "Back to the Trap…even if they having 'Company' without permission," she said sarcastically. "What do we care? It ain't none of our business."

"It's not our business now but it can be," Rocky said. "If we told Yvette and them and they didn't know they may look out for us with a little paper."

Duke sighed and rolled her eyes. "And why would we want to do that, Rocky? Huh? I'm not no snitch. Neither are you. You can keep secrets for years."

"You would do it for me because I asked you." Kisha and Dukes laughed hard, taking a moment longer to simmer down. "Fuck is so funny?" Rocky asked both of them. "Because I'm serious."

"Listen, I know nobody told you so I'm gonna be the one since you my homie and all." Dukes got up from the table and sat next to Rocky on the sofa. "And before you say I'm hating let me assure you that I'm not. I want you to be happy."

Rocky sighed. "Get to the point because you boring me."

"The drug boss ain't gay, Rock. And even if she was she may not be feeling you. I don't know what happened over the summer but that's all I ever hear from you. Mercedes this…and Mercedes that…"

Rocky rolled her eyes. "First off nothing happened. And she don't know what she is or what she likes unless somebody tell her. That's where I come in."

PITBULLS IN A SKIRT

"I know that's what you believe but it's not gonna work this time, Rocky," Kisha said turning the bag upside down so that the crumbs could fall in her mouth. "You may have fucked a few birds in Marjorie but Mercedes is out of your league. So just leave it alone so you won't embarrass yourself."

"Let me school you on something," Rocky started. "Sexy women...and we can all agree that Mercedes is sexy..."

Kisha and Dukes shrugged, neither having much to say on the topic since they were straight.

"...love to explore their sexuality," Rocky continued. "They like to dibble and dabble in all sex has to offer to be sure they are fully satisfied. And without being with a woman, Mercedes can't say that for sure. That's where I come in."

Dukes laughed. "See, that's where some gay chicks get it fucked up, just because I'm sexy doesn't mean I want to fuck a woman."

"Not trying to hurt your feelings but I don't find you that sexy," Rocky said. "I'm just being one hundred." She raised both her palms up playfully.

"Fuck you." Dukes hit her in the arm.

"I said no so stop asking," Rocky giggled and they all laughed harder.

"No, seriously, I'm not with all of this extra shit because I think our lives are heavy enough with the drama," Dukes added. "But, I will say I've been trying to get Lil C's fine ass to notice me from the moment the rental office gave us the keys to our apartment. And if I can get on his good side by snitching to his mother then I'm with it or whatever." She pointed at Rocky. "Even though it goes against my good nature."

"Since we stating our price I got a proposition too." Kisha said rubbing her belly. "Give me your snacks and I'll walk with you to their apartment. I'm in for a little adventure myself today."

Rocky grinned at them sinisterly. "Guess we all getting what we want after all."

CHAPTER SIX

CARISSA

"I'm not gonna answer some dumb shit like that."

He was perfect but even better when he was asleep. I loved looking down at him when he was this way because he didn't fight me. He was just here, peacefully sleeping and allowing me to be in his presence.

When I saw a fragment of strawberry candy on the corner of his mouth I grabbed a washcloth I used to clean his hands off the dresser and wiped it off his tiny lips.

"What the fuck is wrong with you?" Mercedes asked as she entered my room. "Huh? Why you doing dumb shit when the boy's sleep? Does that make any kind of sense to you?"

I dropped the cloth on the side table and stood up. "Get the fuck out my face and my room, Mercedes.

You don't need to watch me when I'm with him." I tried to walk around her toward the door and she blocked my path. "Wait, you want to fight again don't you? 'Cause I'm getting the impression you be rubbing your pussy after I beat your ass or something."

Mercedes gave me the ugly laugh. Like I was a joke. "I'm gonna ask you a question and I want you to be honest. As a matter of fact if you gonna lie don't say shit at all."

I walked closer to her. "What is it, Mercedes?"

"Are you still using drugs?"

I swallowed the lump in my throat. "What...I...what you..."

"You thought I didn't know that you use to do coke with Kenyetta?" she grinned. "Huh? You thought I was that stupid? You move too loosely, Carissa. So stop."

I closed my mouth, as my mind tried to find the right words to say. In all of the time I snorted I never assumed that anyone knew or that anyone would call me on it outside of Kenyetta and she's not here anymore. "Mercedes, stop making up shit."

PITBULLS IN A SKIRT

"They use to call you and Kenyetta the Powder Puff Girls." She shook her head. "Bet you didn't think I knew that."

That was true.

When Kenyetta and me use to do our thing some people did find out and that's the name they gave us. It didn't bother me as much as it did Kenyetta. I guess Mercedes knew after all. Still, it didn't mean I would admit to it either.

"And you wonder why I don't want you around Ryan alone," she continued. "Look at the expression on your face. Of course I know about your little habit. You're a gross ass drug addict. You barely have skin on your bones."

"Mercedes, first of all you come into my room, without knocking and then ask me am I using drugs." I paused. "I been in the gym which is why I'm thin. And you see my face like this because I'm fucked up in the head by your accusation. You know what...just get out because he's sleeping and I'm not about to —"

"You haven't answered the question. Are you still on coke or not?"

"I just said I'm not gonna answer some dumb shit like that."

"I never told you this but I'm gonna tell you now, I blame you for Kenyetta dying." She glared. "Had you not got her so coked out, Black Water's Klan would've never got to—"

Suddenly I had an urge to see my handprint etch across the side of her face in raspberry color. So I slapped her and just like that we were back at it again.

YVETTE

My fingertips pressed into the tissue of Heavy's chest as I slid my hips back and forth over his dick. Outside of being naked when I'm by myself, in front of Heavy was the only other place I felt comfortable. Although I'm not necessarily a fat girl these days, I'm thicker

66

than my sisters, Mercedes and Carissa, which always made me self-conscious about my body.

But Heavy never saw me as the other one next to Carissa or Mercedes, he saw me as a sexy woman and even chose me over them when he first met us the day we took over Marjorie Gardens.

Still, I know some people don't want us to be together, mainly my friends. Some might think he wanted me for my money but that wasn't the case and it's my business if he did.

I never reached into my purse when we went on a date. He never hit me for a loan to pay this bill or that one. He took me out and treated me like a woman and for that I will never let him go.

Don't get me wrong, I know it's best to be with a man who's income mirror's your own but where was I gonna find a nigga with millions? Impossible in DC unless they were in the game and I was not interested if they were.

So I reached for a nigga who cared about me and I think I made the best decision with Heavy.

"Damn, this pussy tight," he said biting the corner of his lip. "You see what you do to me?" He pushed into me again and together we created a sexual rhythm. "My dick hard as iron."

I grinned and continued to work my fuck magic when suddenly I heard Mercedes and Carissa yelling in the other room. If I wasn't preoccupied I would've gotten out of the bed and got them together but I'm getting tired of the constant bickering and I need a break.

That's where Heavy came in and it's the reason I called him to stay with me during the snowstorm.

"Don't worry 'bout it, 'Vette," He said gripping my waist harder. "Don't get off this dick to see about them. They good."

He was right and I felt my pussy heating up and pulsating when I focused on the way he looked at me. There was no way I was about to argue with them when I was on the verge of cumming so I pushed into him more. For a second he clasped my waist so strong I thought it would break and I didn't care if it did, just as long as he stayed inside of me.

"Vetteeeeee, fuck...."

"Heavy, hit this pussy, baby." I bore down harder into his chest with my fingertips and squeezed my inner walls to massage his thickness. "I want you to cum all in this pussy."

"You want this shit, bae?"

"Want all this dick," I said as I whined longer and harder.

"Oh yeah, bitch?" He slapped my ass. "That's how you feel?"

"I love it when you call me that shit. Now take this pussy, Thick."

His eyes widened when I said Thick's name but he didn't move right away.

Fuck!

What is wrong with me?

So STUPID!

Please let him not have heard me.

Instead of responding we continued to press and grind into each other until we both reached ecstasy. When I was done my face pressed into his damp chest as my breathing settled down. I noticed I didn't hear them fighting anymore but heard other voices.

The ones going on in my head.

That made me feel guilty for calling him another man's name.

"Who is Thick?" He asked.

"Nobody," I lied. I rolled off of him and lay on my side. "I was just feeling the moment that's all."

He frowned. "Yvette, if you made a mistake let's talk about it. But please don't act like you didn't call me by another nigga's name."

I blinked a few times. "You hear that shit? In the living room?"

"So you really gonna change the subject like that?"

"I'm serious." I paused. "I hear other voices out there."

He sighed. "'Vette, you know 88 and Fresh in the living room." He yawned. "Maybe that's who you hear. They be alright though. You fed them niggas before we eased off. What more they want? Plus you not their bitch. Besides, I want you to answer my question. Who is Thick?"

I listened harder. "No, I'm serious." Needing an escape to avoid his question, but really hearing voices, I eased up and slipped in my jeans, bra and grey t-shirt on my dresser. "I gotta see what's up. I'll be back in a second and we can talk about all that then."

PITBULLS IN A SKIRT

I opened the door and closed it behind me before he could respond. With my arms crossed over my chest I was surprised to see two black chicks and a white girl in our apartment next to the front door. Mercedes, Carissa, 88 and Fresh surrounded them, preventing them from going further.

What was going on?

The night was getting stranger by the minute.

I broke the semi-circle and walked closer to the girls. One was white and chubby with French braids running down her back, the other had two Afro puffs and the third was really pretty with straight fire red hair. She was also wearing red scrubs and a badge that read *Janelle Monroe RN*. They looked like some strange singing group at first glance.

"They've been frisked already," Fresh said. "No weapons."

"Who are you?" I asked the girls. "And what you doing in my apartment?"

"Exactly," Carissa interjected. "I told Mercedes not to let them in, 'Vette, despite the so called information they claim to have for us. And what does she do?" She looked at Mercedes and rolled her eyes. "Let them in anyway. Stupid shit."

"If we causing problems we can just go," The white girl said. "It ain't that deep and I'm hungry anyway."

"Hold fast," Mercedes told her before focusing on Carissa. "First off I'm a grown ass woman and second—"

"Mercedes, please," I said cutting her off from arguing with Carissa. "Not now."

She took a deep breath and so did I.

Focusing on the girls I said, "My friend said you had some information. So what you got to say?" Fresh and 88 moved closer, touching their weapons just in case. "Whatever it is make it quick. Your lives are in danger."

The one with the scrubs stepped out of the pack. "My name's Janelle but my friends call me Rocky, this is Kisha"—she pointed at the white girl—"and this is Dukes. We—"

"Maybe you don't understand what make it quick means," I said. "Save the fucking side talk for your friends and get to the point. You in the danger zone right now."

PITBULLS IN A SKIRT

Rocky cleared her throat and for some reason looked at Mercedes and back at me. "My bad. We came over to tell you that we saw some chicks walk into the Trap and we – "

Angry that this bitch assumed she knew me I stepped closer to her face, cutting her off. Whoever this whore was she didn't know shit about my business or where I kept my trap houses. And for her disrespect she suddenly had three guns aimed at her hair, each man preparing to make that scalp redder. "I think you over stepped a little, Reds. Might want to turn around and get the fuck out while you still can."

With hands raised, white palms in my direction, she took a deep breath. "Sorry, Yvette. I'm not coming to start trouble. I just got word that the Trap was on the same hallway where we live. I knew you wouldn't want anybody outside of Kliyo and Quinton there so I figured I'd let you know."

Something was off with our management.

Why do folks know where the Trap be?

At first I thought she was some young dumb bitch trying to gain favor but the names she called were correct. Kliyo and Quinton were in the Trap and I specifically told them not to have anybody in that apartment.

"I can't believe we listening to this shit," Carissa said shaking her head. "I think you should put these bitches out of our crib or out of their miseries, your choice. Whatever happens don't say I didn't warn you." In kid mode, as usual when she didn't get her way, she stormed off, slamming her bedroom door behind herself.

Ryan started crying again in her room.

I sighed and focused back on Rocky. "If you lying to me, you get one call to the one you love most. Then you're done in this lifetime." I pointed at her.

I saw the lump crawl down her throat as she swallowed. "Yvette, ya'll been looking out for Marjorie since you been here. Between the community functions, the daycare center and the stuff ya'll do for the kids, all I got is respect for all of you. And I wouldn't play like this. If it's okay that them girls are in the Trap I'll leave right now and you won't ever see me again. It's just that I heard you ran a strict shop." She paused. "Before you took it over there was a lot of grimy stuff going on in Marjorie and a lot of crime when niggas attempted to take over. I'm just giving you information you might find useful. But like I said, we can leave if —"

"You not going nowhere," I said pointing at her. Lowering my finger I said, "Before we check it out do you know these chick's names?"

Rocky shook her head from left to right. "Nope...couldn't see their faces. But one was wearing a red dress and the other a tiger striped one. Oh...they both looked like whores too."

CHAPTER SEVEN

HEAVY

"I need you to correct this situation ASAP!"

*H*eavy was wiping his dick with his moist t-shirt when he heard that two females wearing a red dress and a tiger striped dress managed to get into the trap house.

Fucking Grace! He thought to himself. What are you doing?

His teeth grinded together when he considered all of the things he was going to do to her. Although he knew his baby's mother could be a world class freak when she was with him, even he had to admit that the odds of her being in one of Yvette's traps was too hard to believe.

Still he needed proof.

He rushed to his cell phone, made a call and sat bear ass on the edge of the bed. The phone rung once before he went in. "Please tell me you not that fucking stupid, Grace." He whispered in a hush tone.

"What are you talking about?" She said sinisterly. "And why you calling me all of a sudden? I thought we were done. Isn't that what you said to me a little while ago? Huh?"

"Grace, are you some place you don't have no business being?" He looked at the door.

"Wow, word travels fast. I was gonna call you myself. Besides, I tried to talk to you, Heavy. Remember? I begged you not to leave me and you did anyway."

He stood up. "So this is what you do? Work your way into Yvette's spot, while trying to get yourself killed at the same time? Come on, Grace, this going too far. You're moving to territories you aren't versed on."

"I'm trying to figure out who you call to talk about. Yvette or me?"

He took a deep breath. "If I come over there and see your face I'm gonna pull you out by your — "

"You can stop this now, Heavy. I told you that in your apartment. All you have to do is come back to me."

"Bitch, are you crazy!" He yelled. He took a deep breath when he realized he was being too loud. "You can't blackmail a nigga into being with you by committing suicide. Now what you gonna do is get the fuck out of there or I'ma — "

Click.

When he saw she hung up he decided to put on his jeans and make another call. Luckily the person he was reaching answered. The only problem was that it was too loud in the background to hear him at first. "Yo, I'm sick of your fucking cousin, man," Heavy said laying into him. "She gone too far this time and I need you to go see about her for me. Quick."

Wilson laughed. "Wait...I thought she wasn't your problem no more. At Grams last week she said you dumped her. Anyway, fuck she do this time?" He chuckled harder. "My cousin always in some dirt. Getting your pressure high and shit."

"It ain't funny, nigga," He whispered harshly into his cell. His lips were pressed against the handset so close it was almost difficult to hear his vicious words. But he was trying to avoid Yvette from picking up on what he was saying from the living room. "This bitch is about to ruin everything I got going on here and I need that to stop. Now."

Wilson directed his attention to the people inside his apartment. "Hey, turn that music down for a sec." When the background grew quiet he focused back on the call. "This sound serious, Heavy."

PITBULLS IN A SKIRT

"It is, man. I'm not sure what she trying to do but she fucking with 'Vette and them now. All because she can't get a nigga back."

"Wait...she going at the bosses directly?"

"Yeah, man. And since I'm fucking with 'Vette whatever she got going on will mess everything up on my end. I need you to correct this situation ASAP. Are you even in Marjorie?"

"Uh...yeah...in the building one over but I can make it. It'll be hard cause the snow high as shit and still coming down. It's gonna cost you too."

Heavy took a deep breath. "If you take care of this I got you. Money ain't a problem. My bitch rich. I'll get the cash."

"Then consider your problem solved. I'll hit you later with more details."

Heavy sat on the edge of the bed and took a deep breath. One part of him knew it was a mistake to get Wilson involved. He'd been around him long enough to know that he had a tendency of making things worse.

For now, he'd have to wait.

WILSON

Covered with thick winter coats the men stood in the living room.

"So what exactly are we doing again?" Corey asked as he along with Wilson and Spotter loaded their guns. "One minute we smoking weed and the next we going to the trap to get your cousin and some other bitch. I was hoping to kick back and – "

"Well we not kicking back," Wilson said cutting him off. "All we doing is going over there to find out what she's up to. Plus I just got into the mix with 'Vette and them. They finally put me on payroll with a package last week. If whatever Grace doing gets out of hand how I know the family will be safe? The last thing I need is Grace fucking up my shit too."

"Good, because at first I thought this was about you doing a favor for your cousin's ex-nigga," Corey said with an attitude. "I was gonna ask why you making this our problem."

Wilson shook his head. "Even if I did don't act like you weren't gonna go anyway. We both know what's in it for you." He paused. "Like I said we just checking things out at first."

"So why we tooling up again?" Spotter asked raising his gun. "Seems like a lot of artillery for a question session."

"Because we crashing a party," Wilson said. "While I don't have a problem smacking the shit out of cuzo and her friend, I may have to lay down one of them niggas if they feeling some kind of way about it. It's better to be safe than dead."

"So what you think going on for real in the Trap?" Corey asked. "Because me and Grace set up many niggas in our day and made a lot of money. If she's involved it's gotta be payday related right?" He tucked his .45 in the back of his jeans. "Because I won't be opposed to making a few bucks if we can help ourselves."

"I don't know what Grace is into," Wilson shrugged. "She got mad when I wouldn't let her hold five hundred for rent the other day and I haven't spoken to her since. Don't think she'll want to see me tonight either. But that's her problem not mine."

They all laughed and walked out the door.

CHAPTER EIGHT

GRACE

"It's been a lot of fun too. And will continue to be fun if you go with the flow."

*A*fter round three of the Sex Fest, Grace sat on top of Quinton's dick on the floor, while Kliyo, finished with the fuck games, rested his head in Rambler's naked lap. Rambler fucked him so hard an hour ago that unlike his man he couldn't handle another bout.

Looking up at her, Quinton squeezed two handfuls of Grace's breasts and grinned. "I feel weak. You're wearing me out and we gotta pace ourselves. It's only day one. We need to last for the next two days." He slapped her ass. "What I do to deserve this visit?"

She wiggled her hips on his limp penis and grinned. "Does it matter what you did? We just had sex three times in a row. You should be kissing my feet."

"You fine, ma, got a face fit for a magazine. But I don't do feet. I don't care how wet and tight the pussy is."

Grace looked at the dog food bags on the floor in the kitchen and was almost certain there were drugs inside. The plan was to take the drugs out and to Heavy's apartment hoping to lure him out with a phone call.

"You will once I lay this pussy on you again." She playfully punched his face softly. "I'm vicious with my game. And by the smile on your face right now I know you agree."

He chuckled but his expression turned serious. "I'm not fucking around, Grace. I been trying to get inside this box for weeks and you been crying Heavy's name hard. Even said if I was the last man in DC and looked like Idris Elba you still wouldn't fuck a nigga. What changed?"

She sighed and rolled her eyes. "You too smart for your own good you know? I hate when niggas talk themselves out of the pussy instead of going with the flow." She rolled her eyes. "Just enjoy yourself for now."

She moved to kiss him again and he put his hand in her face.

She frowned.

"First off I already got the pussy." He shrugged. "And being too smart comes with the territory. Now...I'm still waiting on you to answer the question."

"Let's just say I'm using you in my own way." She smiled and ran her hand down the side of his face. When Heavy got irritated in the past she used the move to calm him down but it didn't seem to be working with Quinton. *"Our time together has been a lot of fun too. And will continue to be fun if you go with the flow."*

He frowned. *"Fuck you mean you're using me? And to go with the flow?"* He lifted her off his waist and sat up. *"I'm about to smack the shit out you."*

She perched next to him. *"You look upset."*

"I am…and in a minute I'm about to punch you in the fucking face. Square in the nose."

Grace stood up, slipped into her dress and bra. Her breasts still stood at attention so the undergarment was a nuisance more than a help. *"I meant just what I said, Quinton. I have a purpose and I needed your assistance. You've done that and I would say thank you except I don't think it would matter to you. Let's just drop it and chill out for a little while."*

Embarrassed he stood up and approached her. *"I want you out of here right now, bitch."* He paused. *"I'm not fucking around. I should've known you were weird. What kind of slut wears a summer dress in a winter storm?"* He pointed at her nose. "*And if I see you in Marjorie after this I might lay you down for the disrespect.*" Suddenly letting her in the Trap seemed like a bad idea and he wanted her gone, Rambler too since he was making a list.

Grace laughed totally unmoved by his anger. "*You see, I'm not gonna be able to do that. In fact I'm gonna need 'you' to leave.*" She looked back at Rambler who was sitting on the sofa silent observing the awkward scene. "*And you can take your friend too.*"

His eyes widened and his mouth opened and closed before opening again. "*You got five minutes to –* "

Grace raised his gun and shot him in the forehead, quieting him for eternity. He didn't know she lifted it off of him during sex and now it was too late. Afraid, Rambler pushed Kliyo's head out of her lap and rushed over to her friend. "*What the fuck is wrong with you? Why did you just shoot him?*"

Kliyo rubbed his tired eyes and gasped when he saw Quinton on the floor trying to suck air into his lungs. "*What is happening?*" He asked her. "*What the fuck!*"

Grace smiled at Kliyo's anxiety before looking at her friend. "*Heavy called earlier and threatened me. A little later this cell phone was ringing off the hook. He already know we in here before we could move the package." She snatched it off the floor, where she and Quinton lay earlier. "When I was fucking Quinton and asked who was calling he said the Plug and that he would call her back later. It's time to escalate my plan."*

Rambler rubbed her throbbing temples before sliding on Kliyo's shirt. It was the quickest thing she could use to cover her body and Kliyo was too concerned with his friend to care at the moment.

"You not making sense and you never said anything about murder, Grace." Rambler's heart thumped in her chest as she ran her hand frantically through her short golden hair. "You're all over the place. That's not our area of expertise."

"I did what I had to," Grace shrugged. "For now just relax and let me figure things out. So we can make it out of here alive."

Kliyo, realizing his friend was gone rose off the floor and made a move for Grace. "Bitch, are you fucking — "

Kliyo's words were cut short when Grace aimed at him. "If you think I'm gonna let you talk to me any kind of way you crazy. Now I didn't want to kill your friend but he was about to toss me out and I can't have that right now."

Kliyo raised his hands as his eyes widened. "Okay, okay...can you at least tell me what the fuck is going on?" He looked around for his gun and didn't see it. "Are you robbing us or something?"

"I'm doing whatever I want. And don't worry about looking for your weapon, baby boy, I hid that too." Grace said. "And I'll tell you what's going on. I'm gonna hang out here for a little while and if you get in the way of my plans you'll be reunited with your friend sooner than you realize." She lowered her gun. "In spirit of course."

There was a firm knock at the door.

Grace aimed at him again. "Who the fuck is that?"

"I don't know." His eyes widened as he saw his life flash before him as he considered it being Yvette. "Fuck! Stop pointing that thing at me."

Grace frowned. "Watch his ass," she said to Rambler as she backed up, gun still trained on him. Once at the door she looked out of the peephole. She sighed and lowered the weapon when she saw her cousin on the other side. Along with his two friends. "Fuck you want, Wilson?" She said to the door. "Go home!"

"Bitch, open the fucking door," he yelled. "We done walked over here from the next building and I'm freezing. Jeans wet and everything."

She tucked her gun in between her titties, opened the door and crossed her arms over her chest. Wilson, Corey and Spotter pushed their way inside as if they had rights. Removing their heavy wet coats and tossing them to the floor.

"I hear you were having a party," Wilson said locking the door before rubbing his palms together and licking his lips. "I decided to check it out. I hope you don't mind."

Grace rolled her eyes. "So instead of coming to see about me himself Heavy sends you. That's mighty weak on his part don't you think?"

"I don't know 'bout all of that," Wilson shrugged. "What I wanna know is why you in the Trap?" And then he saw the half naked corpse on the floor. His eyes widened and he covered his mouth with his cold palm. "Please tell me you didn't just do this shit." He pointed at Quinton's body. "Are you crazy?"

"So you want me to lie?"

Wilson relieved her of her weapon and slapped her so hard he temporarily blinded her on the right side of her face.

"I just got in good with them bitches!" He pointed at her using the barrel. "Do you know how long it took me to get on the squad? And what you do? Fuck your way in and kill one of their soldiers. How you think shit gonna pan out for me? For our family?"

"I didn't ask you to come over here!" Grace yelled holding her throbbing cheek. "Blame Heavy!"

"Had I known you were committing murder I would've told him to fuck off. Now just like somebody saw you two bitches coming in, they may have saw us too." He tucked her gun in the back of his jeans with the rest of the weapons. "I hate to admit it but I'm in this now."

"Nigga, we need to leave back out of that door and act like we didn't see any of this shit!" Spotter said grabbing his coat and Wilson's. "Let's roll." He shoved Wilson's damp coat into his chest.

Wilson snatched his jacket and tossed it back on the floor. "We lost any other option the moment we came in here, man."

"Plus I'm not leaving empty handed, Spotter," Corey said as he looked at Grace from the corner of his eyes. "Wilson's right."

PITBULLS IN A SKIRT

All Kliyo and Rambler could do is watch as their lives unfolded before their eyes.

"Exactly, now slide that nigga in the room," he told his men. "I have to figure our next move out."

CHAPTER NINE

MERCEDES

"This feels off."

Yvette stood in the middle of the floor with her cell phone on speaker. We were on our way to the Trap to investigate the girls when Kliyo called and Yvette dug into him. "Nobody's in here, 'Vette," Kliyo said. "I promise. Whoever told you that shit is straight lying."

"That's not what I'm hearing." She paced in place. "I heard two bitches walked in the spot 'bout a hour ago, Kliyo. I thought I was clear on no whores being in the trap."

"On everything, 'Vette, nobody's here." He continued. "If you want to come by you can but I'm being honest. It's just me and Quinton. We ain't opened the door since we been on duty."

"First off I know I can come by and I will." She glared. "And if I find out you lying to me, Kliyo. You gonna have a painful night." Yvette hung up.

PITBULLS IN A SKIRT

"I don't know about this, Yvette," I said as I held Ryan who was moving around nervously in my arm. "This feels off."

"I agree with Mercedes," Heavy said. "Maybe you should fall back for a second. If you want I can go check things out."

Yvette frowned. "You never been involved in my business so you won't start now." She ran her hand down her face. "Listen, I just got my business back on. I'm not about to lose it all on some dumb shit. Right now I have to think things through. Just give me some time" She walked away.

I walked into the hall bathroom where Yvette stood washing her hands. We had bathrooms in our bedrooms so I thought that was odd.

"Why aren't you in your room?"

"I needed to throw some water over my face real quick."

I leaned against the doorframe. "Are you thinking what I am?" I asked as I watched her run a clean wet washcloth over her face.

She took a deep breath. "I'm thinking a lot of things, Mercedes. Be more specific and help me out."

"You don't think they could be tied up into this in some way do you?"

She took a deep breath, turned around to look at me. "Karen and Oscar led a sheltered life in the Black Water Klan. They stayed amongst themselves. Plus we swept Marjorie before taking it over. Nobody here was affiliated."

"Then what is this about?" I asked in a hushed tone. "I'm so sick of being hunted and having to look over my shoulder. This can't be how life really is. Do you realize it's been years since I've had a good nights sleep."

She laughed. "I'm not having them now."

"I'm serious!"

PITBULLS IN A SKIRT

She looked up at me. "Mercedes, I'll take care of this, I always do. Just give me some time to sort all of this out." She walked around me and out the door.

I was trying to put Ryan to sleep who was agitated by the noise and negative energy when Rocky walked inside the room. I looked back at her and grabbed the gun on the bed before aiming at her head. "Fuck you doing in here? You don't just come in my room."

Rocky threw her hands up. "I'm sorry. Didn't mean to intrude. I was coming from the bathroom and it looked like you needed help." She swallowed. "I can leave if—"

I know the girl was no threat since they were checked for weapons earlier so I placed my gun down where I could grab it if necessary. "No, you can come in," I said cutting her off. "Maybe a face that doesn't get on his nerves will calm him down."

Rocky smiled, walked inside and sat on the edge of the bed. She looked over at Ryan who was still fussing, picked him up and placed him on her lap. Then she slowly massaged his temples in small circular motions.

Ryan wiggled for a few seconds and went silent.

I smiled. "Wow...I...it worked..." I took a deep breath since his screeching voice stopped. It always put me on edge when he was in a bad mood. "Usually I can get him to settle down but today he seems different."

"He probably senses something's wrong. Babies have a sixth sense." She looked down at Ryan and back at me. "I'm sure he does know something is off. There's a lot going on in Marjorie apparently."

"I heard that too." I focused on the technique she was using for future references. "I really can't believe that's working."

"My grandmother use to do this to me all the time. And to all of her grandchildren and her great-grandchildren too. Even when we were older she'd do it if we had a headache and it always made it go away."

I sighed. "Well tell her I said thank you when you see her again."

Rocky's disposition saddened as her shoulders hunched forward. "I would if her young boyfriend didn't kill her when she stopped giving him money two years back." She sighed. "And since my mother died three years before her murder, with liver cancer, we never recovered. I'm the only one who uses this technique on people."

Wow. I wish I hadn't said anything about her grandmother.

"I'm sorry to hear about your family," I said as I watched Ryan drift into a deep sleep. "Can't imagine what—"

"Fuck you doing back here?" 88 asked Rocky, causing Ryan's eyes to fly open before he started crying again. To make shit more intense he had his weapon trained on her. That might not have been so bad if she wasn't holding my blood relative.

"She's fine," I said turning toward him, placing my hands on his muscular chest, which moved up and down with heavy breaths. "Now put that shit away, you scaring Ryan!"

88's eyes remained on Rocky although he tucked his weapon in the back of his jeans. Finally he looked down at me and stomped out the room.

"I'm sorry," Rocky said massaging Ryan's temples again, putting him at ease. "You want me to leave? I would go home but Yvette said she wanted us to stay here to keep an eye on us."

"No...stay with him. I'll go talk to 88."

I rushed out of the room.

88 seemed draped in total whiteness as he paced the balcony, which was dusted lightly with snow due to being partially covered. I walked out to greet him with

his jacket in my hand. The snow making scrunching noises under my fresh Timberland boots.

I was already wearing my chocolate fur coat to battle the brisk weather.

Closing the door I handed it to him and looked back into the apartment to be sure no one was watching us. When I didn't see anyone I took a deep breath. "Now you know why I said we should've never started with each other."

"Hold up, you mad at me?" He pointed at his chest. "She wasn't supposed to even be back there. She said she had to go to the bathroom and the next thing I know she's sitting on your bed. Can't you see that girl is gay, Mercedes?" He put his coat on angrily. "You do have eyes don't you?"

I laughed and held my stomach. "And what the fuck does her being gay have to do with me?" I frowned. "You know I don't go that way and never will. You need to relax." I paused and looked into the apartment again to be sure we weren't being watched. "Now what's this really about?"

"I'm sick of competing, Mercedes!" He walked a few feet away from me before approaching me again.

"First Jackson and now this bitch." He pointed into the apartment. "It seems like everybody can get a piece of your time but me."

I looked into our crib and up at him again. "You're coming undone and you need to keep your fucking voice down, 88. If they find out we been sliding off it may get back to C." I moved closer so that he could see my eyes. "And trust me...neither one of us wants that to happen. He'll never approve us being together. You know that."

"I'm in love with you, Mercedes. Do you understand what I'm saying? I'm in love. And I'm sick of sneaking around, fucking you in your Bentley and public parks like you a whore."

I smiled hoping to lighten the mood. "I thought you liked having sex that way, said you appreciated the excitement. Said it was refreshing to be with a boss who knew what she wanted." He was glaring and I could tell he wasn't there for my seduction game so I took a deep breath and changed my approach. "Come on, 88...you knew I had a man before we started. Why you changing now?"

PITBULLS IN A SKIRT

He walked a few feet away from me and grabbed the sides of his head before dropping his hands at his sides. "You have to decide what you want, Mercedes. And you gotta decide now." He pointed at the snow-covered balcony floor.

"What's there to decide? Outside of Jackson and me living together I haven't let him touch me in months. I'm not that kind of woman and I want you! I told you that already."

"I'm not talking about fucking you. I'm talking about us making it official. Either you're willing to be my woman or I'm done with all the games. Do you want that?"

What was it about me being attracted to men I was in charge of? First Derrick and now 88. Maybe I feel safer if I held their financial power in my hands. When I was with Cameron he owned me before we took over Emerald. I didn't want to be vulnerable again.

I walked up to him. "Come on, 88, don't do this to me. If you walk out I have nothing else. You are my excitement...don't take that away from me right now."

He pushed me away softly. "Are you not hearing me? I got feelings for you and I'm getting the impression that we'll never move forward. Either you want me or you don't. I told you how I feel. It's your choice not mine." He stormed off the balcony, leaving me alone.

From where I stood I could see Heavy leaving and I wondered where he was going. 88 walked over to Fresh who stood next to the door and they seemed to be talking about Heavy's quick exit.

I didn't see Yvette so I figured she was still trying to decide what to do. Should we go to the Trap house or not to investigate this whore situation? Personally I was apprehensive because even though we knew a lot of people in this building there were many more we didn't know.

It could be a set up.

And what if Karen and Oscar were involved?

All the Trap thoughts went out the window because I had something else to deal with, when I stepped off the balcony Carissa was standing before me, grinning. I closed the door, tossed my fur coat on the back of the chair and looked at her. "Fuck's so funny, bitch?"

"A lot." She crossed her arms tighter over her chest. "For starters I wonder how Lil C will feel when he finds out you fuckin' his friend. One of his good ones at that."

I moved in closer, hoping to scare her into submission. It's not like it worked in the past but it was at least worth a try. "Don't fuck with me, Carissa. You don't know what you're talking about and I advise you to leave it right here and right now."

"You mean how you did when you accused me of using drugs a little while ago?" She paused. "And what do you mean by don't fuck with you? Huh? I'm not afraid of you, 'Cedes. I'm not worried that you'll do something to me. Your muscle is my muscle. Your soldiers my soldiers, so you can't bully me into being quiet. So step the fuck off."

"You see, that's where you fuck up. You think so small." I pointed at my head.

The smile wiped off of her face. "What's that supposed to mean?"

"Don't you realize there are a number of ways I can get at you? And the best part is you'll never see any of them coming."

Her eyes widened before she glared. "Hold up...you threatening my kids? I know you not that crazy!"

"All I'm saying is this...I am not your enemy, Carissa, unless you make it so by telling my son a bunch of lies." I moved closer. "Now stay the fuck out of my business, before I change your world in ways you can't imagine."

"Wow...that must be some really good dick to have you turn on me." She shook her head.

"You made it this way remember? I did all I could to show you how much I appreciated you choosing Lil C over Persia. But I'm done kissing your ass, Carissa. Like I said, stay out of my fucking business or you won't have a choice."

I stomped away.

CHAPTER TEN

CARISSA

"We talk in code all the time and suddenly you can't understand me?"

Something is going on and I don't know what. It's that feeling of when the world seems like it's closing in on you all at once.

Death is in the air.

I feel it in my bones.

I wanted so badly to do a line or two of coke but I didn't have access to it since I got snowed in and was unable to get to my stash. Not only that but with Mercedes watching me I had to be careful.

Still, coke was the only thing I could have to help me deal with this shit. I need to get to the Trap house and steal a bump or two but how would that be possible?

After getting into it with Mercedes I walked up to the huddle at the door, which included Yvette, 88 and Fresh.

"I don't know what this is about but ya'll have the wrong impression about him," Yvette said. "Heavy would never do anything to hurt me. I know him."

"Yvette, I understand that he's your man but where's he going?" Fresh said. "Why would he leave the apartment when there ain't nowhere to be but here? DC is on lock."

"Not that I have to answer to you but he's going to his place." She shrugged. "Said he had to grab something out of his apartment right quick. It's not like he doesn't live here."

"Don't get me wrong, I've never heard about anything foul about Heavy. He's been standup as far as I'm concerned." Fresh pressed on. "It's just that I saw the look on his face and it didn't sit right with me. He was frazzled and we need to play things close right now."

"I'm not trying to alarm you, 'Vette but Fresh is right," 88 interjected. "I heard him talking on the phone and he sounded like whatever was going on had him heated. Maybe I should walk over to his crib to check on him."

"No!" Yvette yelled. "Ya'll not about to turn this situation into something it's not. Now I said everything's cool so leave it at that. The only thing on my mind is that pack in #745 and the possible whore situation."

"Have you talked to Kliyo again?" I asked, folding my arms over my chest.

"Yeah...he answers the phone and everything but something is up, Carissa. My mind is so tossed up that I can tell if it's a set up or the FEDS fucking with us. Trying to lure us to the apartment to pin a major rap on us." She looked at everyone. "So excuse me if I don't wanna talk about Heavy right now." She stormed off and I followed.

I was almost in her room when she slammed the door in my face. I opened it anyway and shut it once I was inside. I watched her open and close drawers looking for only God knew what.

"You miss him don't you? In your mind Heavy is him and you are still in love."

"Miss who, Carissa?" She tossed around a few t-shirts. "You always talking in code."

I laughed. "You are very smart and intelligent, Yvette. We talk in code all the time and suddenly you can't understand me? Yeah right."

She froze, faced the wall and sighed. "Don't fuck with me right now, Carissa." She turned around and looked at me. "I'm not in the mood as you already know."

"I notice something about you. You're attracted to men who remind you of him." I walked deeper inside even though she wanted me gone. "And although you get warning signs you ignore them all hoping to get one more moment of when you weren't in charge. You claim to like being the boss, the one we all go to for help, but I think you resent it too. Deep down you want nothing more than to curl up in a man's lap and have him tell you what to do. Aren't I right?"

She giggled. "Says the woman who hasn't had a man in years."

I laughed despite the sting I felt from her harsh words. I didn't know if it hurt because she was telling the truth or the latter. "I don't want a man. Besides, I don't have any good role models around here to inspire me. Because you and Mercedes are all in fucked up situations."

"Oh really?" She grinned, grabbed a pair of strawberry socks from the drawer and sat on the edge of the bed. "I wouldn't need a man either if I favored cocaine."

My eyes widened.

"Oh yes, I know about your little habit too, Carissa. This is why nobody wants you around the product and why we have to keep eyes on you at all times."

"So what you saying?"

"You aren't trustworthy. The only reason why we still keep you around is because if we took hands off you we're afraid you'd turn into a full-blown addict. Embarrassing the hell out of the Emerald City legacy." She paused. "So do us all a favor and stop acting like your high and mightier when you're crack whore low."

For a moment I lost my thought. She was talking to me like I was a Head or something.

Not trustworthy? Up until this moment I never knew my trust was in question and I felt queasy.

"Yes, I do favor coke every now and again. And yes I'm not proud of it but it doesn't make me dumb."

"Correction, it makes you an idiot, Carissa. We see what that shit does to people who go too far. Why fuck with it at all?"

"It's funny how the supplier downs the customer." I shook my head.

"Don't turn this around on me."

"You know what, maybe I need an escape! Ya'll prefer dick I do a line or two!" I took a deep breath. "And we've never been the same. Since Lavelle, Cameron, Thick and Dyson died we've been torn apart." I shook my head. "We don't even talk about losing Kenyetta no more. She was our sister, sat on the steps with us in Emerald City every day and we disrespect her memory by not talking about her. Why?"

Yvette put on her socks. "Not everybody wants to wallow in pain but it doesn't mean we don't miss her."

"That's a fucking excuse."

She jumped up and approached me. "What the fuck you want me to say? That I wonder if having all the money in the world was worth losing Thick?

Despite how he treated me? Or that I wonder if Kenyetta forgives me in Heaven for not doing everything in my power to save her life before she got with Black Water? What you want me to say?"

"I don't want you to *say* anything, Yvette. I just want you to *feel something*, before it's too late for all of us. And the next person dies."

She walked away and flopped on the edge of the bed. "Stop talking like that. Nobody else is dying. Not unless you and Mercedes kill each other with all the fighting." She took a deep breath. "Speaking of conversations, if you want to talk about keeping this family together you need to start with mending the relationship with her instead of wasting your time with me."

I frowned. "She hates me."

"She doesn't hate you, she's just hurt. You blame her for the decision you were forced to make to kill Persia." She paused. "And I know losing your daughter hurts to this day but it wasn't her fault. She wasn't responsible, Carissa."

"I think whatever relationship Mercedes and I had is officially over. And I'm not gonna lie, I think about the million ways the world would be better off without her sometimes. I know it's wrong but I'm expressing my soul."

She stood up and stomped toward me. "And if you ever express your soul like that to me again we will no longer be friends." She pointed in my chest. "I'm talking I'd better never hear you call my name on the streets or I will kill you. Now get the fuck out of my room. I wanna be left alone. I got some pertinent shit to think through."

CHAPTER ELEVEN

GRACE

"If I spelled shit out you still wouldn't get me. So stop trying."

*G*race sat on the edge of the bed and stared down at *Quinton's body when Corey walked inside the room with his hands stuffed in his pockets. Although it was once her plan to step into the Trap she soon realized she was not in control anymore.*

Plus the cell phone had been ringing non-stop with Yvette and Kliyo was forced to lie repeatedly that things were okay when they weren't. It was just a matter of time before things kicked off and the Pitbulls came hunting.

Corey walked deeper into the room and sat next to her and stared down at the corpse. "Why you kill this nigga?" He pointed at the body. "It's gonna start stinking up the place in a few hours. You ready for that shit?"

113

She rolled her eyes. "Corey, just get the fuck out." She stood up and walked toward the window, pulling the blinds up to look at the snow like a tomb surrounding the building. "I swear all the niggas my cousin fuck with are stupid."

"I'm serious...why you ain't let me in on your plan?"

She looked at him and back out the window. "Just leave me alone. The last thing I feel like doing is talking to you. Besides, if I spelled shit out you still wouldn't get me. So stop trying."

He frowned. "You act like I'm the problem."

"What the fuck do you want, Corey?" She stomped toward him. "I got a lot on my mind and you not helping matters right now."

He took a quick breath. "How many jobs have we done together? How much money have we taken from niggas we robbed? Not one time have I turned my back on you. And now you got a plan and didn't – "

"This not about money, Corey! It's deeper than that. Much deeper." She walked across the floor and leaned against the wall. "And it's worth more to me than you can imagine."

He stared at her and his head tilted sideways. "So you telling me that you really broke into a trap house, killed a *nigga and have it not be about running off on the plug? Are you sick or something?"*

"No, it's worse. I'm in love, Corey." She sighed. "And I realize that concept don't make sense to you but it's the world to me."

He chuckled. "Who you in love with? Heavy's beefy ass?"

She rolled her eyes. "Who you think?"

"But that's the nigga who sent us here. Told us to drag you out by your hair if we had too." He paused. "Trust me, when he gave the word it didn't sound like he gave a fuck about you. It's time to get over him, Grace. Don't you think so?"

She sighed. "I know how he feels about me whether he says the truth or not. He loves me. He really does. What I don't understand is why he wants to forget us so badly? It's like he's so wrapped up in this bitch that he doesn't see me anymore. We have a child together."

"Had a child."

"Don't disrespect me or my daughter." She frowned. "Let us not forget the body on the floor in this room. Understand that I did that shit right there and won't have a problem doing it again for greater offenses." She pointed at

115

him. "My daughter may be dead but she's still my daughter."

"I haven't forgotten that you murdered a nigga or whatever. I'm just confused on why you care about a dude so much that don't love you back."

"I know why you saying that. You still want me…"

"So what." He shrugged. "Since we talking about it lets get it out in the open. I fucks with you, Grace and wanted you to be my woman. But the only thing you see is Heavy."

"He understands me."

"He don't fuck with you no more! Why I gotta keep repeating myself?" Corey's voice rose and he grew ballistic. "And everybody in the city knows it too. You playing yourself like a fool." He stood up and walked toward her. "Don't you think it's time to get that through your fucking head?"

Suddenly there was a knock at the front door. Hearing the sound Grace and Corey rushed out of the room only to see Heavy in the living room going off on everybody with ears. When he saw Grace he rushed up to her, grabbed her shoulders, and squeezed tightly. "What the fuck you doing here, huh? Are you really trying to sabotage everything I've built?"

Grace wiggled out of is grasp before he snatched her again. "So this is what you do now? Hurt me?"

"Bitch, you doing this just to get at me and you leaving right now!" He rushed her to the door and she pulled away from him. Slowly he turned to look at her. "You testing my patience."

"I'll leave if you want me to, Heavy. All you have to do is take me back and tell Yvette you chose me."

He placed his hands on both sides of his head and squeezed. "What the fuck is wrong with you? We not kids, Grace. You don't get to act out when you don't get what you want."

"I'm not acting out!" She cried. "All I want is us back together. How things use to be. Say you'll be with me and I'll stop all of this."

"NO! WHAT I'M GONNA DO IS SNATCH YOU OUTTA HERE!" He lifted her up, tossed her over his shoulder and moved toward the door.

Wilson, Corey and Spotter quickly closed in before he could exit. "Put her down, man," Wilson said calmly, although his request sounded more like a threat. "Now I know you got problems with my cousin but she's still family. And the only person gonna be handling her like that is me."

Heavy frowned, placed her down on her feet and glared at all of them. "This is not making any sense." He looked at Grace. "Do you know what them bitches can do to you? You not being smart...none of you. Right now they're trying to decide if they should storm this spot or not. Is that what you niggas want? There are much easier ways to kill yourself you know. And less painful ones too."

Wilson frowned. "Storming us?" He said to himself.

Kliyo on the other hand looked as if he was about to throw up. His stomach had been sour ever since Quinton was murdered and he was farting every five minutes, causing the room to smell like blue cheese and boiled eggs. "So...so Yvette don't believe me that nobody's in here?"

"What you think, slim?" Heavy asked.

Kliyo stood up. "Man, she's gonna cut off my dick! I...I gotta go to the bathroom." He rushed away, slamming the door behind himself.

Wilson shook his head and everyone focused back on Grace and Heavy.

"This wasn't about Yvette and them until you made it about that. This is about you abandoning me," Grace cried. "All I wanted was your love."

PITBULLS IN A SKIRT

Heavy looked down and sighed. He didn't have room for any emotional games but if lying would get her out of the apartment that was what he was willing to do. He took a deep breath and prepared to lay down the game. "Okay, Grace. You got your way. If you leave with me, and everybody else too, I'll tell her I want to be back with you."

Grace's eyes lightened up. "For real, Heavy?"

Corey stepped closer. "This is cute and everything but we not gonna be able to turn around so easily now. Things have gone to the next level." He was beyond jealous while witnessing Grace's heartfelt confession. "We gonna have to see this through and Grace gonna ride it out with us, fam."

After taking a loose shit Kliyo walked back into the living room. Holding his belly he said, "I don't mean to be annoying but can somebody tell me what the fuck is going on now? What are you niggas really doing here? One minute I was sleep after getting some pussy and the next more niggas I don't know are in the Trap. And these bitches stole my gun." He frowned at Grace and Rambler. "What is happening? I mean what's happening? Are ya'll robbing us or not? If so take the bricks and go."

"At this point you should do your best to fall back and stay out the way." Grace frowned at him. "Before you end up like your man in the next room."

Rambler sighed. "So what is the plan now?"

Wilson, who obviously took the lead, stepped closer to everyone. "We make the most of the situation." He suggested. "All of us." He looked at Heavy. "If you ask me the new plan should be to find a way to get the Keys out of this building unnoticed." He paused. "But the back door is locked and even if I walked the product to our building everybody will see me. We have to think clearly before moving."

"Is everybody in this bitch fucking crazy? There is no way they letting you leave this building with their coke." Heavy yelled. "I don't want no part of this shit."

"That won't work now, Heavy," Wilson smiled. "Sadly enough. Even if you threw us under the bus nobody will believe you weren't involved. Grace is your daughter's mother."

Grace walked up to him. "It's true, Heavy. You might as well stay with me and – "

"I said I don't want no part of this!" He yelled looking at Grace, Rambler, Wilson, Corey, Spotter and Kliyo. "Now are you coming with me or not, Grace? I'm not gonna keep asking."

Graced moved to respond when Corey shoved her a few inches back. "I already answered your question for her, man," He interjected. "Maybe we should show him the body in the room. That way he can really understand the gravity of this situation."

Heavy's eyebrows rose. "Wait...ya'll in here killing niggas too?" He placed both hands on the side of his face before dropping them. "Are you serious?" His eyes widened.

"Correction, she killed somebody," Wilson said pointing at Grace.

"Who did she kill?" Heavy continued.

"Quinton, one of their soldiers," Corey responded.

"You know what...whatever you niggas do is on you. Just leave me and my name out of it!" He stormed out of the Trap, slamming the door in the process.

"He's gonna be a problem," Wilson said looking at the door. "Should've never let him inside."

"I can tell him to come back so we can hit him with something if you want, Wilson," Spotter suggested raising his gun.

"Don't fuck with him," Grace yelled approaching Wilson. "Everything happening is my fault and Heavy don't have nothing to do with it."

"I'm with Wilson," Rambler said. "Are we fucking with Heavy's head so you can be with him, Grace? Or are we robbing the bosses? 'Cause this don't have nothing to do with what we talked about earlier today, G. Your nigga came to get you, like you wanted. But you didn't go. Why not?"

"Bitch, ain't you listening to me?" Wilson yelled stepping to her. "Every plan before I got in here is dead. The only thing we should be doing now is trying to figure out how to get those kilos out of here when that snow melts. And since our names are all over this shit, we need to also be thinking about how to kill them bitches before they kill us. Because trust me it's coming. You heard, Heavy." He turned to look at the dog food bags. "Wait, I have an idea!"

CHAPTER TWELVE

MERCEDES

"You good with talking about why a plan won't work but you've never been part of the solution."

Yvette stood in the middle of the floor with me, Carissa and 88 behind her. She had a cell pressed to her ear while frowning. "Fuck, nobody answering the phone now!" She tossed it on the couch. "I'm sick of this shit."

This entire ordeal was making me all kinds of mad. Prior to Rocky and them coming over we never had any reason to suspect Kliyo and Quinton of foul play. They've worked with us for months and we trusted them.

Well...somewhat anyway.

And now it was as if all of that was being tossed out the window.

"This nigga answered his phone every time I rang him and now he ain't got no time for me?" Yvette looked at all of them. "And where's Quinton?" She scratched her scalp. "It's settled, I gotta go over there." She moved to the closet and grabbed her fur jacket because the hallway was cold.

So cold you could see your breath when you spoke.

"Wait, Yvette, before you do anything let's talk it out," I said. "We haven't fully gone over the *what if it's a trap* scenario. And I think it's worth our time. Don't you? Karen and Oscar are out there?"

"I'm going to get my kilos," Yvette said.

"And where you gonna put it, Yvette?" Carissa asked. "Here? So we can go down like the Spanish-Jamaican cat out New York?" Carissa shook her head from left to right. "You know DC police been trying to get at us for years, Yvette. We have to play this smart. Ain't that what ya'll always tell me?"

Just then my phone rang. I took it out my pocket and looked at the number. "It's C." I answered and put it on speakerphone. "Hey, son, I got you on speaker."

"What's up, fam?" Lil C said out loud. "Everyone holding up?"

Everyone collectively said, *Yeah.* But it was obvious we weren't.

"No flight out yet?" I asked. "Because we need you back now."

"Nope, and it don't look good. They expect at least seven more inches in DC. Man, all I'm trying to do is come home." When his voice sounded a little irritated I took the call off speaker and walked toward the balcony. I figured he wanted a little privacy. Looking out the frozen door I asked, "How things going? 88 and Fresh still there right?"

I looked over at 88 who was staring at me before looking away. I was worried someone else would see me. And catch our glances.

"Yeah, but something's up, Cameron." I paused. "Kliyo and Quinton not answering the phone. It don't look good. I think they may be turning on us."

"I knew something was up, I could hear it in your voice. I hate this shit happened with them new niggas. Like I said, they were loyal but neither of them were responsible for this much weight." He paused. "Let me wrap to Fresh right quick, ma."

I walked over to Fresh and said, "C, wanna talk to you."

Fresh jumped up and took the call. "Boss..." He walked away, out of earshot from the rest of us.

I rejoined Carissa and Yvette who were both agitated. I could tell the tension was building and it was just a matter of time before things exploded. "Like I said, I'm going over there," Yvette said nodding. "I gotta know what's up and I gotta know now. Waiting is killing me."

"Look, instead of you going, maybe I should," Carissa suggested.

Yvette looked at me and we both laughed. If she think somebody would have her cokehead ass around the pack she was crazy.

"You can't be fuckin' serious. Since when do you answer the call for shit like this? You're usually the last person who wants to go."

She crossed her arms over her chest tightly. "What's that supposed to mean? You calling me a punk?"

"It means exactly what it sounds like, Carissa." I continued. "You good with talking about why a plan won't work but you've never been part of the solution. *Ever.* And I don't see any reason you should start today. So do yourself a favor and fall back as usual."

Carissa knew she had never been the fighter type and with her on drugs she was even more laid back, unless she passionate about something or trying to get her point across.

It's amazing that after all of these years, she still resembles Salli Richardson with her copper-colored skin despite her habit.

Still she always allowed Yvette and me to handle the problems on the streets since niggas gave her the most shit because she was short and petite.

Carissa frowned. "What is it really with you?" she asked me. "We fight all the time but you been coming at me extra hard lately, Mercedes. Just be honest."

"Like I said, stick to what you know. And when it comes to handling the tough work me and 'Vette got it. You know that already."

Yvette's cell rang just as Carissa was about to say something to me. Whatever it was it was probably stupid.

"Kliyo, why you ain't answer the fucking phone a few minutes ago? I been hitting you." Yvette yelled into the handset. I couldn't hear what was being said until Yvette put the call on speaker. "Hold up, what did you just say to me?" she frowned.

"Quinton's dead, boss," Kliyo said. "He died from an overdose. I'm sorry...I didn't know what else to do so I called at the last minute. That's why I wasn't answering the phone."

Everyone gasped.

It was at that time that I remembered that Rocky, Kisha and Dukes were still in the apartment. I looked back at them but they were doing a good job of pretending not to listen. Their backs were turned toward us and everything.

But who wouldn't eavesdrop on this shit?

"Fuck you mean he overdosed?" Yvette yelled at the handset. "You telling me that ya'll niggas been fucking with my shit?"

I turned around and saw Fresh had moved closer. He had my phone in his hand and was holding it up in the air. I'm sure so Lil C could listen.

PITBULLS IN A SKIRT

"I didn't know he was gonna do it, 'Vette," Kliyo continued. "I took a nap and when I woke up he had dug into one of the packs. I don't know what to do now," Kliyo whined. "I'm not trying to be snowed in with no corpse, man." His voice grew more frantic. "You gotta come and help, boss. I ain't never been in a situation like this and I'm all alone."

Yvette's face turned red. "Stay put. I'll hit you in a second."

"But you gotta come now, 'Vette," Kliyo persisted. "I'm not trying to be in here alone!"

"Nigga, don't tell me what I gotta do. I said I'll hit you back."

"Okay and I'm sorry again. About everything," Kliyo continued. "I didn't know he—"

Click.

Yvette hung up on him before he could finish his sentence. I've seen her angry before but never this mad. Her face was almost blue like she was holding her breath but I understood where her anger stemmed from.

We just got back on and something like this could set us back financially.

129

Our plug wasn't gonna give us product on credit anymore. We needed the cash up front which meant we needed the pack untouched.

"Are you trying to tell me this ain't no trap, 'Vette?" I yelled. "I'm telling you something's up and we shouldn't make any moves until we thing things through."

"I'm with, ma," Lil C said from the speakerphone. I almost forgot he was listening. "This is what we gonna do. Fresh, I want you to go see what's up at the Trap."

"No problem, boss. You want 88 to roll too?" Fresh continued.

"No, I want him to stay with my mother and aunts." Lil C responded. I was relieved too. I cared about 88 too much and until I knew exactly what was happening I didn't want him anywhere near the spot. "Hit me back when you know something more."

Lil C hung up and Fresh handed me my phone. Fresh was preparing to walk out the door when 'Vette stopped him. "I know what C said, but I don't think you should be going by yourself. Let me go with you."

"Fuck is wrong with you, Yvette?" I paused. "Don't you know when to fall back and delegate? We not on

130

the steps of Emerald no more. Ain't no reason to bust your gun when we have soldiers."

"But he don't need to be going by there alone," Yvette said. "I got a feeling about this shit."

"I'll go," Rocky said. "I mean...I know how to use a gun and I'll watch his back."

"If ya'll let this bitch go with him to the Trap I'm gonna smack the shit out everybody in this room." Carissa roared. "I don't even understand what they're still doing here."

Part of me agreed with Carissa. But Yvette felt it best to keep them where we could see them instead of letting them leave. That way if something else was going on, and they were in on the alleged Set-Up, Rocky and her friends couldn't alert Kliyo and Quinton of our plans. Also, there was something about Rocky that I liked.

She was genuine.

Her energy makes me feel like I can trust her and you don't get to be in our business long without being able to read people.

"Let her go," I suggested. "Since Lil C wants 88 to fall back with us."

"You know what...both of you bitches are getting dumber by the snow flake," Carissa stormed toward the back of the apartment just as Heavy knocked on the door.

Yvette let him inside and he walked up to her. I don't know about everybody else but the first thing I noticed was that he wasn't carrying a bag. So what did he get from his apartment?

And why did he leave so abruptly?

"Sorry, it took me longer than I thought." Heavy said before kissing Yvette on the cheek. "But can I talk to you for a minute? In private?"

She looked at all of us and then back at him. "Yeah, baby, sure, let's go to my room. "They walked away and collectively everyone appeared to have the same expression.

Nobody trusted the nigga Heavy anymore.

At one point I was on his team but with everything going on and his shaky personality I couldn't call it.

Fresh dug in his waist and pulled out one of his guns which he handed to Rocky. "Are you sure you know how to shoot? 'Cause ain't no need in you hanging with me if you can't bust back."

"I'm at the range every weekend." She laughed. "Trust me, I got your back."

"She not lying 'bout that," Kisha said eating a bag of Kit Kats. We said she could have *some* food but she was drying us out. There were hardly any snacks left but nobody was going to deny a pregnant woman her grub either. "Even when it's her weekend to grocery shop she at the range. She definitely can shoot. You'll be good."

I rolled my eyes at her fat ass and focused on Rocky and Fresh. "Go to the trap, see what's up and come right back," I said. "If you see something off don't play the hero. We'll deal with it when the snow breaks."

"No problem," Fresh said.

ROCKY

Fresh and Rocky crept down the hallway leading to the Trap house. "So you got a man?" Fresh asked her. "Somebody who you feeling when times get rough like now?"

Rocky laughed. "Not that there's anything wrong with it but it's not my thing."

He chuckled. "Fuck that 'spose to mean?"

She shrugged. "Don't know how to make it clearer than I already have. You asked a question and I gave you a direct answer. Men ain't my thing."

He shook his head. "Women have just given up on trying now a days." He sighed. "One nigga breaks their heart and they run to the other side."

Rocky laughed. "First off I was born this way. Not into the fads like you may think. But fuck all of that. Let's just do this job Mercedes asked us to do and head back. To be honest I don't see how my private life applies to the current situation anyway."

"We gonna do that. I was just trying to pass the time. But let me tell you something else too...you're cute. And if you ever want to come back home I'll be more than happy to greet you."

"Wow. Didn't take you for a jerk."

PITBULLS IN A SKIRT

He laughed quietly. "I'm just putting my bid in that's –
"

"I saw something," Rocky whispered touching his arm.
They were six apartments from the trap at the end of the hall.
"You see that shit? Somebody moved."

Fresh removed his weapon but it was too late. They were
suddenly bombarded with bullets flying in their direction.

CHAPTER THIRTEEN

CARISSA

"I need some air, I'll be back when I feel like it."

There was a loud banging on the front door just as I came out of my room to get something to drink. Sensing something was off; I rushed to the door with everyone else behind me. Before answering I glanced out the peephole and was shocked to see Rocky covered in blood.

BANG! BANG! BANG!

"Open the door, please!" She yelled, causing the door to rattle with every pound.

I turned around and looked at everyone. With my back against the door I whispered, "It's that girl ya'll sent with Fresh and she got blood all over her scrubs. She look like a serial killer or something."

PITBULLS IN A SKIRT

Mercedes stepped up, her eyes as wide as melons. "Well open the fucking door." She moved toward me and touched the knob but I shoved her backwards. "We not letting that woman in here. Are you fucking crazy? I just said she looks like a serial killer."

"Carissa, stop messing around. If she's covered in blood she could be hurt." Mercedes continued. "Now open the door."

"Plus I need to know what's going on with Fresh, boss," 88 said to me. "If you want I can go out there and find out myself before letting her inside."

"No!" Mercedes yelled. "I mean...I mean..."

I grinned. "Don't want your lover boy getting hurt do you? Isn't that special."

"You know what, Carissa..." Mercedes charged me and knocked me to the side before opening the door. She was so rough I almost hit my forehead on the table at the door side.

Before I could fight back the door was wide open and Rocky collapsed on the floor while breathing heavily in front of us. Fresh lie at her feet and blood poured from the multiple wounds on his body.

"What the fuck just happened?" Mercedes asked as 88 and Dukes helped pull Fresh inside safely.

I slammed the door behind them and looked down at the bloody scene, just as Yvette and Heavy came out of the room and rushed up to us. "What the fuck happened?" Yvette yelled. "Why is he shot?"

Rocky raised herself up but only to her hands and knees. Looking up at us she said, "We were almost to the spot when...when...they started shooting at us. It seemed to be coming from everywhere. From all directions. So...so I used the elevator to drag him here." She was trying desperately to catch her breath.

"Who was it?" Yvette asked while 88 and Heavy tended to Fresh's bloody body.

"I couldn't tell but I think it was coming from the Trap." Finally she stood up and leaned on the white wall, leaving bloody smears everywhere and some other places too. "It was hard to tell. We let off a few rounds but they outnumbered us. Even from other apartments too...well...I think. It was all happening so fast."

"Out of other apartments?" Mercedes yelled. "What you mean?"

"There were a few doors before you reached the Trap, and they opened and started shooting," Rocky continued. "I can't tell you which doors opened but it was an ambush for sure."

The more she spoke the angrier I got. If they couldn't tell this girl was involved in this shooting I was afraid they never would. "I can't believe ya'll buying into her shit." I advised. "The Trap is probably overthrown and now we got Fresh in here who may die in any moment."

Mercedes rolled her eyes. "Carissa, just stop—"

"Don't tell me what to do!" I yelled pointing at her. "We need to either kill these bitches or put them out before they turn on us next." I said referring to Rocky, Kisha and Dukes. "You even had the nerve to authorize giving Rocky a gun, 'Vette."

Yvette scratched her head. "Oh yeah, take Rocky's gun until I figure everything out."

88 quickly relieved her of her weapon and Fresh's who she was also holding.

Slowly Yvette walked up to me. "Now that, that's done what you gonna do is chill the fuck out. Getting extra excited about things won't help us. Don't forget about what happened with the Black Water Klan. Making quick moves without thinking is why we lost most of our men, Carissa. And your daughter."

That was a low blow.

"You know what, I don't trust nobody in this apartment!" I yelled. "And don't blame me when you find out I'm right about trusting people." I rolled my eyes. "I need some air, I'll be back when I feel like it." I grabbed my white fur coat out the coat closet, even though I probably wouldn't be able to open the building's door to go outside due to the snow. "But it's not like anybody cares anyway."

"So you gonna go outside after they got shot?" Mercedes asked.

"Shut up!"

"Stupid, bitch! Always clasping for attention. Sit your boney ass down!"

I moved toward the door and 88 jumped in front of me. "I'm sorry, boss, but I can't let you leave. I hope you understand. Things are too busy out there right now. Look at Fresh."

I frowned. "Nigga, you better get out of my face before I hurt you."

"I wish I could move out your way," he continued. "But C said I wasn't to let you guys leave the apartment." He paused. "If you want me to call him I'll—"

I was about to take my coat off because at least he cared.

"You know what...just let her go," Mercedes said waving her hand. "If she want to walk down the hallway when we're being hunted maybe she deserves to die. I'm sick of her shit."

"But C said—"

"88, just let her go," Mercedes said firmly. "We have to tend to Fresh."

I rolled my eyes.

As usual, nobody gave a fuck about me.

I stormed out of the apartment.

CHAPTER FOURTEEN

YVETTE

"His fate is already chosen," I said. "But yours has just begun."

I stood over Fresh's body whose breath was getting weaker. He was lying on Carissa's bed as blood poured from his wounds and dampened the mattress under him. As I watched his breath weakening I was still having a hard time believing that all of this was happening to us. We were close to Christmas and it was supposed to be more festive.

Yeah right.

I turned around to look at Mercedes, Rocky and 88 who were also in the room. "He's not gonna make it," I said.

"I know...what we gonna do?" Mercedes asked.

"We can't call 911," I said. "Even if they could make it through the snow to save him it would bring a whole lot of questions with it." I walked to the other side of the room and sat on a chair. "I wonder who's doing this, Mercedes. We need a plan."

It was at that point that I realized I had said the same thing repeatedly. *Think of a plan. Think of a plan.* Where I was use to making decisions in the past quickly, it was like I was doubting myself now. Basically not trusting my own direction.

It wasn't all my fault.

The last time I made big decisions Carissa's daughter was killed.

All I wanted was to be careful.

"What are we going to do about Carissa?" 88 asked. "I really don't feel good about her being out there by herself. C told me to keep eyes on all three of you. Want me to go look for her?"

"No!" Mercedes yelled. "And stop asking!"

Rocky and me looked at her.

I took a deep breath. "Rocky, leave us alone for a minute. I have to rap to Mercedes and them right quick."

"Sure...no problem, Yvette." She walked out and closed the door, allowing me to focus on the secret couple.

"If Lil C finds out both of you are fuckin' each other he's gonna stage a war in the family." I whispered not trying to disturb Fresh. "Now I don't want to get into the details of how wrong this is and on how many levels. I know you know already. But trust that he will go off."

"We aren't fuc—"

"Mercedes, please don't lie to me," I said stopping her game. "It's not necessary and it won't change what I know to be true. I don't have a problem with it but we both know C will."

Mercedes sighed. "It's not like that. We just spend a little time together that's all."

"*A little time together.*" 88 laughed. "On that note I'm gonna wait out in the living room. To guard the door and what not. Let me know if either of you need something." He stomped out.

"Wow, *and* he's in love," I said as I witnessed his mood. "Got a young nigga shook do you?"

"Yvette, please don't..."

"What you gonna do about Jackson, Mercedes? You started a whole 'nother relationship when you haven't even ended it with him. How you think that's gonna play out?"

I shrugged. "Are we really gonna talk about this now?" she said. "Must I remind you we have a half dead man in our midst. Can we work on one thing at a time? I'm begging you."

We both looked at Fresh.

"His fate is already chosen," I said. "But yours has just begun. Be careful with that man, Mercedes."

"Don't worry, it's about to be over. I care about 88 but I can't be what he wants me to be now, 'Vette." She moved closer to Fresh. "Especially with all of this going on." She took a deep breath. "What we gonna do about the Trap?"

"At the end of the day nobody takes nothing from us, Mercedes," I said firmly. "Nobody. So we gonna attack. Storm the Trap."

Heavy came into the room. "You need anything, baby? I can get—"

When my phone rang I looked down and shook my head. "It's Carissa." I grinned. "Ain't been five minutes and already she calling." I put the phone on speaker. "Yeah, Carissa. You realize what the world already knows? That you're snowed in and can't go no fucking where like the rest of us? Just come back here please. Before somebody snatch you."

"You won't be laughing when I tell you what I found out."

My expression grew serious. "What is it?"

"Somebody you won't see coming is involved in all of this mess…"

"Stop fucking around and tell me who, Carissa!"

"It's Grace," she said. "I saw her open the door a few minutes ago. Now will you believe me when I say Heavy's involved?"

Gut punched, I looked at Heavy who sighed.

CHAPTER FIFTEEN

YVETTE

"The only thing on my mind is my coke."

I stood in front of Heavy in my bedroom trying to understand how or why Grace would be tied into all of this. Not only that, while Carissa was talking suddenly we heard a noise and the call went dead. Since she wouldn't answer her phone when we tried to reach her back we weren't sure if she was hurt or if the call just died.

I knew I needed more men so I had Lil C send two more soldiers from around Marjorie who were not necessarily working with us, but not against the regime either. The pickings were slim and he needed all the help we could get. It was hell getting over here and Heavy gave them warm clothes to replace their wet ones.

They were in the living room waiting on my orders.

But first I had to deal with Heavy.

"What is Grace doing in the Trap, Heavy? Huh? She fucking with my shit or something?" I frowned.

He approached me and touched my shoulder but I walked away. "Don't put your hands on me. Ever. Because you lying to me, nigga. And I want to know why."

He stomped to the bed and flopped down. It groaned a little under his weight. "I'm gonna answer your question, but first I need to know if you think I would be capable of hurting you? In any kind of way?"

Silence.

"Yvette, is that the type of man you think I am? One who would share your bed and then hurt you? If Grace is in the Trap I don't have nothing to do with it. I'm done with her. You know that."

"Don't try to turn this around."

"Baby, Yvette...I...I..."

"Don't say those words," I said crossing my arms over my breasts. "Even if they're true if you say the words right now I'm gonna think you're doing it because of everything that's going on. It won't feel genuine. Tell me you feel that way when the time is different."

"Saying the words now doesn't mean they're not true. I love you, Yvette." He got up and walked toward me. "When my daughter died I thought I would go with her. I didn't want to be around anybody or anything and you stepped up in ways I didn't think possible."

I sighed. "Because I didn't want you alone."

PITBULLS IN A SKIRT

"And I don't want to be alone now. Yvette, baby, whatever Grace got going on, whatever she's doing…is not my doing. Do you hear what I'm saying? Because you're rolling your eyes while I'm talking. I'm trying to tell you that I'm not a part of whatever the fuck Grace got going on."

"That may be true, Heavy," I said looking up at him. "Right now the only thing on my mind is my coke. Even if I had a pocket of time for this type shit I couldn't do it now."

Mercedes walked into the room. "I know you know 88's friends are out here." She looked at Heavy and rolled her eyes. "We waiting on you, 'Vette. Let's go and handle business."

"Mercedes, I know you don't believe me but—"

"I can't stand Carissa sometimes," Mercedes started cutting Heavy off. "We fight a lot and it makes me not want to be around her most days but if something happens to my friend and Grace is involved I will burn down this building and everybody you've ever loved, Heavy. It's important that you know that." She stormed away.

"Fuck!" Heavy yelled punching the air. "This bitch is fucking up everything I'm building with you. Even got your friends thinking I'm a snake."

I looked at him opened my mouth and walked out. Words felt dumb right now.

I cared about Heavy and I haven't cared about a man as much since Thick but the same traits I found attractive in Thick were the same ones that existed in Heavy.

A lot of mystery and unanswered questions.

I had to be smart.

Right now there's one thing on my mind.

Getting my coke and friend back safely.

88

88 walked up to Fresh's bedside and looked down at him. Rocky who was a RN had redressed his bandages with cloths made out of clean sheets since she didn't have any more fresh gauze available. But it was obvious that no matter what she did he wasn't going to make it.

Rocky looked as if she wanted to cry as she gazed down at Fresh's bullet battered body. In her mind she bared some responsibility and it was fucking with her head. "I'm sorry, 88, I...I...I tried to – "

88 raised his hand. "Don't say anything," he told Rocky. "Just leave us alone for a second."

She walked out and closed the door.

Fresh opened his eyes and looked at his friend before closing them again. In a voice so low it was almost inaudible he said, "You need to tell C, man about you and his mother. Don't let him find out another way."

88 smiled and walked a little closer. "This nigga on his last breath and he using it to get into my business. It's so like you. Controlling stuff to the end."

Fresh smiled, although his lids remained sealed. "You right, nigga. I may be dying but I'm not trying to see your face too soon when I'm in the afterlife. Just 'cause you fucking with C's mother."

88 rolled his eyes and stuffed his hands into his jean pockets. "I was just fucking around about you dying. You not leaving me too soon. You could still make it with – "

"Over shawty's house, in that old white Volvo without the plates, there's a box full of money. About $90,000. Divide it between her and my mother."

"Come on, man..."

Fresh groaned, the pain from the bullet wounds he suffered reminding him that he was on borrowed minutes. "I don't have a lot of time to beg you, 88. I asked for something and I need you to follow through. Can I count on you?"

88 sighed. "Yeah, my nigga."

"Good. Now let me get my rest," Fresh continued. "I'm gonna need it."

YVETTE

"Carissa, what you talking about?" I paced the area in front of the door just as 88 walked into the living room after sitting with Fresh. "One minute you hang up and the next you calling like everything is cool. Where are you?"

"I'm on my way back in a little while, 'Vette," she said. "Nothing's wrong though."

152

I looked at my friends. "This doesn't make any sense." I continued. "Where were you when the call ended? Why we hear that loud noise in the background?"

"I said it was a misunderstanding! Leave it alone!" She yelled. "Oh, and you should come to the Trap. I'm gonna check some things out and I want you to come with me. But come by yourself. We don't need a big parade or nothing."

My eyebrows rose and I looked at Mercedes. Someone was forcing her to say these things. "Oh really? Come by myself? Why?"

"No major reason, 'Vette," Carissa said. "I just think everything is okay at the Trap and I thought you wanted to check on it too. Now come on. You can bring Mercedes but nobody else."

"Yeah...aight...I'll do that." I ended the call and tossed the phone on the sofa before running my hand down my face.

"She's clearly lying, Yvette," Mercedes said. "But what we gonna do because you not going by yourself?"

"I don't mean to be rude but is there anything left to eat? I'm hungry." Kisha said insensitive to our friend being in trouble.

Irritated with her insensitivity, Mercedes grabbed her by the hair, dragged her to the door and removed a set of keys from her pocket. "88, there's a supply closet across the hall, throw her ass inside."

He grabbed her by the arm. "No problem."

"Please don't do this!" Kisha screamed rubbing her belly. She did that every time she asked for something to eat. "I'm scared of small places and I'm with child."

"We put niggas in there before. There's a pillow and blanket inside, you'll be alright for a little while."

Kisha looked at Dukes and Rocky as 88 dragged her out.

Thinking her friends were gonna jump I looked at them.

"I'm gonna check on Fresh," Rocky said walking to the back.

"And I'm gonna help Rocky," Dukes said following her.

I guess her friends were tired of her too because they left her hanging.

Mercedes walked up to me and said, "Even if Carissa's lying we still have to get her. She won't survive in a heated situation long."

I took a deep breath and looked back at our new additions, Scott and Vance, two of Lil C's men. "Do you know much about Kliyo and Quinton?" I asked them.

"No, Yvette," Scott said. "But I heard Quinton use to rape chicks."

"I heard that too." Vance said.

"Well if it's true that he overdosed we might not have to worry about him," I responded. "Kliyo, on the other hand is a problem. Do you think either of them have manpower?"

"Nah, outside of your men they be by them selves around Marjorie," Scott said. "They can't summon nobody that'll want to get involved with your set."

"What about Grace?" I continued. "Who's she related too?" I could've asked Heavy but I had a feeling he was gonna fake dumb. He stood behind me and looked sick to his stomach.

Vance and Scott looked at Heavy. "All I know about her is that Heavy use to deal with her and that her cousin is Wilson," Scott continued, throwing Heavy under the bus as politely as possible. "A native from Marjorie who I think keeps time with C's squad recently. And some underground niggas who can't be trusted."

"Yeah...I know." I paused before looking back at Heavy and then the men. "Okay, we have to get inside the Trap. The thing is the metal door is reinforced with a security bar. We had the door made so it couldn't be kicked in as easily. Now it would cause us more problems than it's worth."

"I got something for that." Vance said. He walked toward the door where a large grey duffle I noticed earlier sat. Slowly he kneeled down and removed a few high power guns and then a huge black battering ram. It took some work to lift it up but he showed me. "Don't ask how I came across this but let me be clear. With this in our arsenal we'll get through any door. Even the Trap."

Lil C chose the right niggas.

And all I could do was smile.

CHAPTER SIXTEEN

MERCEDES

"Sometimes a girl wants a lie or two."

The apartment was almost completely silent. There was no announcement to grow quiet but everyone seemed to be thinking about the same thing. That we were moving out in two hours and needed a moment of peace.

Carissa called back several times to ask where Yvette was and each time Yvette gave her a different ETA of when she would be coming. We knew they were using her to get to us but we would not move out on their time. It was clear that she was being held against her will.

And I was going to get her.

I was putting on some fresh socks because the floor was wet due to everyone coming in from outside. 88 walked into the room and standing next to the door said, "So there's nothing I can say to convince you to lay here. And to let me and them dudes handle this?"

157

I smiled.

He walked deeper inside. "I'm serious, Mercedes. Fall back on this one. You don't have to go to every war."

I sighed and touched the side of the bed next to me. "Sit down." He walked in and flopped down on the mattress. "I don't want you to save me, 88. That's not what we're about."

He shook his head. "What is it about powerful women?"

"I'm confused."

"If I said nothing and let you deal with all of this alone you wouldn't have any respect for me. You'd probably call me a punk behind my back and even tell your friends about how I didn't offer to help you. To fight for you."

I rolled my eyes.

"But since I'm genuinely concerned about you and what you going through you look at me like I'm irritating," he continued. "I want to know right now what you want me to do, Mercedes. No more games. Let's put it all on the line while we still can."

"Why are you doing this now, 88? Seriously."

"Because I want a fucking answer." He pointed at me. "I want you to be real with me and since you like to do things under pressure what better time than now?"

I stood up, walked across the room and leaned against the wall. "I told Jackson about us today. I called him and told him how I felt."

"Did you tell him about me?"

"No...I couldn't break his heart. But I think he knows."

88 smiled but removed it quickly. "Well what he say?"

I sighed. "He begged me not to make any decisions right now."

He frowned. "And how do you feel about that?"

"88, I love you. I didn't want to say it like this. With everything going on but I do and it's been a long time since I've felt this way. Since Derrick really. I didn't even feel like this with Jackson."

Looking at him he was a carbon copy of Cameron when we first got together, even his age. Except in this scenario I was six years older and not as confident. Every part of me wanted to let go and experience life with him but what if he left me after I gave him my heart?

He got up and walked toward me. "Don't think too much about it, Mercedes." He put his arms around my waist and looked into my eyes. "I'm only six years younger and you're the only woman I desire." He paused. "I can already see your mind giving you all the reasons why it won't work. I'm just asking you to consider a few on how it will."

"It's easier said than done."

"I know."

I sighed. "You gonna hurt me."

"Even if I do, that's life."

I walked away. "That's not what I wanted to hear."

"So you prefer lies?"

I looked away. "You too blunt. Sometimes a girl wants a lie or two." I smiled. "It makes her feel better."

"But I'm not dealing with a girl. I chose a woman."

I grinned and felt guilty when I thought about what my sister must be going through in apartment #745. Here she was fighting for her life and I was falling deeper in love. "You do know this is the wrong time right? I can't help but say it again."

160

"What else we doing? We can't make a move until the time Yvette chose. And since you're going with us I would be fucked up if something happened to you and I didn't get a chance to tell you how I feel, Mercedes. It's now or never. I just wish you'd let me and the fellas go alone. 'Vette too."

"You made a lot of good points earlier." I paused. "About the kind of woman I am. I do like a man who's not afraid to fight when need be. But just like I'm attracted to a certain type of man you're attracted to a certain woman too."

"What that mean?"

"88, if I was sitting home hitting up your phone every five minutes you wouldn't give me the time of day. You'd be bored out of your mind with our relationship."

"You crazy! I would love that shit."

"You would love it now…with me being who I am. But if I met you like that you wouldn't be attracted to me. Men love women who are inaccessible. Not available." I kissed him on the lips. "At the end of the day we both love danger. So let's bust our guns and explore that part of our personality…together."

"Hey guys, sorry to bother you," Dukes said entering the room. "Rocky wants to see you in Carissa's room. It's about Fresh."

Fresh was barely breathing when we walked into the room and I knew it was a matter of minutes before he died. It wasn't until that time that I realized 88 and Fresh were really close. It was in the painful expression on his face as he stood near Fresh's bedside.

Me, Yvette, Rocky, Heavy and Dukes stood in the background. It seemed like we were eavesdropping on the end of a good friendship. While Vance and Scott remained armed at the front door in the living room in case anybody had a mind to pay us a visit.

Ryan thank God was still sleep.

"He won't make it long," Rocky said wiping her hand on a bloody rag. "I did all I could to stop the bleeding. But...but..."

PITBULLS IN A SKIRT

I saw tears rolling down her face and knew she felt personally responsible for his fate. I guess when we first asked her to help Fresh nobody thought about how she would feel if Fresh didn't make it, which we all knew was a firm possibility the moment we saw his body.

She was a registered nurse not a doctor.

"Let's leave 88 and Fresh alone," I suggested. "They need privacy."

Everybody walked out of the room and I was following until Fresh called my name with a painful breath. I walked up to him. "Yes, Fresh...what do you need?"

"The girl, Rocky, she's gonna take this hard," Fresh said in a light voice. "Kept saying how sorry she was that she couldn't save me. Whatever you can do for her I'll appreciate, Mercedes. It's a dying man's last wish."

I exhaled. "On everything I hold dear with those words she'll never have to work another day in her life. Consider it done."

He smiled and looked at 88. "Make them niggas pay, man. I don't...I don't know who...but watch the…the apartments before the Trap. Watch…watch…them closely. It's…a…"

"Rest, my nigga," 88 said. "And know I'm going for blood."

Fresh smiled one last time and closed his eyes forever.

CHAPTER

SEVENTEEN

CARISSA

"Let me go and we can put all of this
behind us. I promise."

I'm gonna die.

I'm gonna die and I can't fix myself to come to
terms with it by praying, even though that's what I
need to do.

One minute I was walking down the hall to
confront Kliyo since Quinton was supposedly dead
and the next I was being pulled inside of the Trap
house. Forced to lie to my friends and get them to
come here. I knew they were smarter though and knew
they would never come alone. Despite my suggestion.

But things were worse than I thought when I
moved deeper into the Trap house.

When I finally saw Quinton's dead body in the bathroom a few feet from where I lie on the bed I could tell from the hole in his head that he hadn't overdosed. And I knew it was only a matter of time before his corpse would start bringing with it the foul odor of death.

I was about to attempt to take a nap, in the hopes that I could think of a plan to set myself free when the door opened. I knew his name as Wilson because he smacked Grace when he caught her asking me if Heavy really loved Yvette. And if they were gonna make it or not.

As if I knew for sure.

Stupid, bitch!

But I learned a lot after that brief altercation between those two. For starters they were not a complete unit, which meant I could possibly break them up with the right words. I also learned, by the way Rambler took care of me, that she was worried that when the dust settled and my girls came looking that she would be on the wrong end of the battle, which as of now was true.

"How are you?" Wilson asked with kind eyes settling on me. "The binds aren't too tight are they?" He closed the door behind himself. "Because we don't want you uncomfortable."

The more I looked at him I could tell he was a good person, who probably got roped into this by Grace's sneaky ass.

I smiled. "I would prefer if they were off." I sat up and leaned against the headboard, my hands tied in front of me. "You think you can help me with that? I would really appreciate it."

"Unfortunately they have to stay on but I must admit, I hate seeing you like this."

"Well then, why are you doing it to me?" I asked. "I know you work for us, Wilson. Why let them drag you into this when you know what the end result will be? War."

He shrugged and sat next to me. "I'm afraid of them." He looked at the door and back at me. "My friends."

"Well who's in charge?" I asked.

"Kliyo," he said with wide eyes. "Couldn't you tell?"

"Not really. I mean, I know him and he would never do all of this. He looked scared sitting in the corner at the table. And it didn't seem that he was in charge when you slapped that girl for asking me about Yvette and Heavy. " I paused. "If you're afraid what was that about?"

"You got me. It's just that I blame Grace and her friend for all of this. Had they not come in the Trap none of this would be going on. You have to believe me."

"Prove it. Then let me go, Wilson. Let me go and we can put all of this behind us. I promise."

"Why would I do that?" he paused. "So your friends can come in here and kill me anyway?" He shook his head from left to right. "I'm afraid we're well beyond that now and I'll have to let things play out. Whatever that means."

I scooted closer to him. "Listen, my friends are vicious but they're also compromising. If you let me go they'll understand that you had nothing to do with this. Trust me. It doesn't have to go much further than what it already has."

"Is that right?"

I smiled at his innocence. "Yes, if you let me go and I put a word in for you things will be fine and all they want is me to be safe."

"But what about Quinton? If I let you go they'll still blame me for him. After all, one of their soldiers is dead. Nobody's gonna let that ride."

I shrugged. "Well what happened to him?"

"All I know is that I came in after Heavy told me to pull Grace out of here and he was dead." He moved closer. "I don't know what they're into out there but I promise that I had nothing to do with any of this in the beginning."

I shook my head. "Let me ask you something else, is Heavy involved?"

His eyes widened. "Heavy? Why...do you think he is capable of this?"

"My friend is kind of green when it comes to him. She's normally smart about these kinds of things but men always confuse her. Actually my friends Yvette *and* Mercedes."

"You seem like you're smarter than they are." He grinned. "Seems like you know when people are lying and when they aren't."

I smiled. I could already tell he knew me too well. "Yes. I'm a very good judge of character." I paused. "And because of it I can tell that you are in over your head, Wilson. Release me and I promise that my friends will not hurt you. Or Lil C when he gets in town."

He frowned and his jaw twitched. Suddenly his mood grew darker and he looked like a different person. "Lil C huh?"

"Yeah...I know people are scared of him but I got him in my pocket just like the rest of them. A lot of people don't know but him and my daughter had a son together. His name is Ryan. So trust me when I say he listens to me. I'm kind of like his second mother when you think of it." I swallowed the lump in my throat because I could tell he was minutes away from releasing me. "All you have to do is let me go and −."

Suddenly I felt a stinging sensation across my face that I couldn't soothe with rubbing it because of how my hands were tied.

It took me a moment to realize he'd slapped me.

Hard.

PITBULLS IN A SKIRT

While laughing hysterically he said, "I'm sorry but I couldn't take anymore. I had to stop fucking with you when I saw how serious you were about leaving. Talking about you know a nigga's mind and shit."

"What you mean?" My face felt hot and I could feel tears coming on.

"Bitches like you make my balls itch. You think you can speak down to a nigga and that every man will fall into your spell. " He lowered his brow. "Don't you?"

"No...I...uh..." The words felt loose in my mouth and suddenly I didn't know what else to say. Where I was so sure I was going home before we spoke now I wondered if I would leave with my life.

Or my dignity.

He laughed louder. "Let me be clear. My cousin started this shit to get the nigga Heavy back. That part is true. Personally I think it was a weak move on her part because I know how he feels about Yvette or whatever." He paused. "But still, I'm kind of glad Grace made the move."

"Why?" I asked as my lips trembled. "Since you said you weren't with this plan in the beginning."

"The nigga Lil C fucked my bitch last week. I'd been with this girl for a year and he fucked her just because he could. Had her geeking too because he was *'the boss'* as she put it. Thinking he was all about that slut."

"Maybe he didn't know you were with her...maybe he...maybe..."

He frowned. "He knew what he was doing. And he did it because he could. And because of it you gonna do something for me." He undid his belt and I knew what was about to happen.

He was going to rape me.

"I'm begging you...please don't do this...please don't—"

"I'm gonna stop you because you need to understand that there's nothing you can say or do that will prevent me from busting this nut. But don't get me wrong...when I'm fuckin' you if you still wanna say please...no and stop...feel free. It'll be like music to my ears."

"Wilson...you don't have to...no..."

He cut the lights off and had his way with me nonstop against my will for over an hour.

172

CHAPTER EIGHTEEN

MERCEDES

"You getting soft, Yvette?

It was that time.

We were standing in the living room with our guns fully loaded. Rocky and Dukes sat across from us just looking and for a second I wondered what kind of people they thought we were. Did they think we were greedy because we were willing to risk our entire lives for the pack?

But it was the game we chose and we had to see this thing through.

For the moment anyway.

With Fresh dead neither one of them had any real purpose but I wanted to keep Rocky out the way and safe, especially since Fresh asked me to look out for her. I figured no harm no foul in keeping her with us until this war sorted itself out.

Taking a deep breath I looked at Yvette, Heavy and 88 who held the gun power. Vance and Scott held the

173

Battering Ram and were standing in front of the door waiting.

Yvette looked at all of us and said, "Whatever happens don't stop busting until we get Carissa back and my coke."

I nodded. "I'm' not leaving without my girl, 'Vette," I told her. "You don't have to worry about me."

"Me either."

As I thought about what she said I considered all the times I fought with Carissa. It all seemed dumb and trivial now that her life was in sincere danger. For some reason, even when she threatened to leave the apartment, claiming to need some air, I never really imagined she would be hurt or was in any real danger.

What I wouldn't give to take that moment back now.

Yvette gazed at Heavy before looking at us. "Let's move out," she continued.

Ready for it all, we opened the door and took the steps down toward the seventh floor. We moved like skilled shooters as we crept up the cold hallway, guns aimed in front of us. I could hear my heartbeat in my eardrums and everything in me said this wouldn't end well.

But there was no turning back.

We were on a mission.

When we finally reached the door Heavy opened it, aimed out and then peeked out. We all remained still, waiting for the verdict. Were there shooters in the hallway or not? Sweat balls crawled from Heavy's hairline and along his temples as I watched him.

Now that I thought about it, it was probably dumb to have Heavy tell us if the coast was clear, especially since we couldn't be sure if he was involved or not.

It's too late now.

Finally, after what seemed like an eternity, he looked at us and said, "It's clear. Let's move out."

With that we all glided into the hallway with guns pointed outward. Heavy first, 88 second, Yvette third and me last, followed by Vance and Scott with the Battering Ram.

It was then that I realized something else.

On a normal day the seventh floor, like the other floors, would be bustling with kids and people running back and forth down the halls and along the stairwell.

175

But now it was still. I didn't know if we should be worried or appreciative that we could move so easily without additional eyes.

It was as if the building knew something we didn't.

Still, we crept down the hallway, barrels pointed toward apartment #745. The same door that held my best friend and our product. My hand trembled as I continued to point my weapon.

There was something else that I didn't tell my friends.

A secret I held close to me.

It was one of the reasons I came down so hard on Carissa. After today I was leaving the drug business.

Forever.

I'd saved enough money to be done with it all and I wanted Carissa strong for Yvette because she couldn't do it alone. I told Carissa I blamed her for Kenyetta's death but that wasn't the full true story. I was stepping out and she needed to step up. But with her on drugs I knew it would never happen and it angered me even more.

We were halfway to our target, preparing to knock the door down when the apartment doors before #745 opened and two men with ski masks started firing at us. Suddenly all you heard was sporadic pops as bullets fired both ways crashing into walls over our heads and the windows.

"Get the fuck out of here, Mercedes!" 88 yelled as I continued to bust my gun. "I'm not fucking around! MOVE NOW!"

POP! POP! POP!

"NO, I'M NOT LEAVING YOU!" I yelled at the top of my lungs.

"BITCH, get the fuck out of here! This shit is serious!" He yelled louder. "GOOOO NOW! We being ambushed!"

Before I could refuse Yvette snatched me and whisked me back into the stairwell and down the staircase. When we heard a suspicious noise on one of the floors above us, we ran through the doors unto the 5th floor and took the elevator upward. I leaned against her body, barely able to catch my breath. I felt light headed but I didn't know why. It felt like I was observing someone else's life.

Except when I glanced in the reflection of the elevator door this person had my face on it.

In under a minute we were off the elevator and back in our apartment. The moment the door opened Rocky and Dukes rushed toward me, their eyes wide with what looked like fear.

But Yvette put her hand out for them to stand back.

What was going on?

Why was everyone looking at me like I was crazy?

Yvette locked the door and ran through the apartment with her gun drawn. She was being cautious since we left Dukes and Rocky there alone with Ryan who was still sleeping peacefully in his playpen. There was nothing we cared about in there to steal, but since we didn't truly know them, what was stopping them from sneaking someone in there to infiltrate us while we were gone?

When she came back she sat her gun on the table and moved toward me slowly. She took a deep breath, grabbed both of my hands and looked into my eyes. The moment she did I laid into her.

"Why the fuck you pull me out of the hallway? We weren't supposed to leave without Carissa. Remember? And what if something happens to 88! I will never forgive you." I yelled. "You getting soft,

178

Yvette? Is that why you pulled me out? Since when do we leave a war?"

She took another deep breath. "Mercedes...look at your arm. You've been...you've been..."

"What?" I yelled.

"Look at your FUCKING ARM!" she said louder.

Slowly I followed her gaze and when I saw my arm, and the huge gash of flesh hanging I noticed I was shot. "Oh my, God! I...I...been hit!"

"Get over here and clean her up!" Yvette yelled at Rocky. She must didn't move fast enough because she screamed louder. "I SAID GET THE FUCK OVER HERE AND HELP MY FRIEND!"

Quickly, Rocky rushed toward me and hustled me to my room. "Are you in any pain?" She asked as Dukes rushed into the room and ran water in the bathroom sink. I couldn't speak as she led me to the edge of the bed where I sat down, watching the blood pour over my light skin.

Was this a horror movie or my life?

"I'm...I'm gonna...die ain't I? This...this is it?"

"Do you feel any pain, Mercedes?" Rocky asked as Dukes rushed back out with a bucket of warm water and a clean washcloth.

"No...I...I don't understand what's—"

Suddenly I felt dizzy and the room seemed to spin. I couldn't understand what was happening. I saw the hole in my arm but where was the pain? Why hadn't I...

And then it hit me.

All at once.

A blinding searing pain that felt like a ton of hot coals had been dropped on my skin. The feeling was intense and my arm suddenly felt heavy and numb. I could no longer breathe.

I passed out.

YVETTE

PITBULLS IN A SKIRT

I checked on Mercedes who was lying down on the bed, the bullet wound being tended to by Rocky. For the moment Mercedes eyes were closed and she looked peaceful and I hoped she would stay that way. "How is she...how is she..." the words got trapped in my throat.

"I used some needle and thread to stitch her up," Rocky said as she continued to care for Mercedes. "But she lost a lot of blood. We need to take her to a hospital."

"I'm gonna be straight with you, she ain't Fresh. If she dies you might as well kill yourself too. Her death is not an option for me. Do you understand?"

"Ye...yes, Yvette." She swallowed the lump forming in her throat.

I left the bedroom and entered the living room. The moment I closed the door 88 was fighting me to get back to see her but I knew it would be best if she got rest.

"Not right now, 88," I said softly, understanding how he felt. Their love affair may have been short and secret but I have loved her for most of my life. She was my sister and I was doing my best to keep my emotions at bay. "Let Rocky and them get her together. It's best if we stay out of the way so they have room to work."

He sighed. "But is she gonna…is she gonna…"

"She's gonna be fine, 88," I said taking a deep breath, trying to believe myself too. "But you have to let her get some rest. The last thing they need is nervous energy around the situation."

"FUCK! Why didn't she listen to me? I said not to go and she went anyway!"

"You doing all of this ain't helping right now," I said to him. "Put that anger in the right place, 88. Let's focus on getting these niggas back, whoever they are. Now ain't the time for misplaced rage."

He nodded but I could tell his heart was hurting. He followed me as I walked deeper into the living room to get the update on what we needed to do next. After all of this we were sure of two things, number one, we were definitely being hunted and secondly they had more firepower than we did.

PITBULLS IN A SKIRT

I walked up to Vance, Scott and Heavy who were waiting on my word. "So what now, boss?" Vance asked.

"First, I don't want anybody to tell Lil C what happened to his mother before I do. He can't be here right now and I don't want him concerned about something he can't change." I took another deep breath, while trying to push the idea of losing another one of my best friends out of my mind.

"No problem," Vance said although Scott looked away from me guiltily. "I'm not saying a word."

I knew instantly he called Lil C already and could only imagine what Lil C was going through in the moment. "Please say you didn't call C..."

"I'm sorry...he told me to keep him informed and I couldn't lie to him," Scott continued.

"FUCK!" I yelled.

"So what we gonna do?" Vance asked.

"I need more power," I said. "We can't measure up to the muscle they bringing."

"If you not terribly mad at me for calling C and not opposed to dealing with non conforming type niggas, I have just the men for the job."

"But how they gonna get here?" I asked. "The roads are still not plowed. We in a fucking ice tomb right now."

"Luckily for us they live in the building over. Trust me, they'll get here. Even if they gotta shovel and kick." Scott said. "The earth will make way for them that's for sure."

"Get on top of it. Tell them I need them like yesterday." I pointed at him.

A call was made and thirty minutes later I heard some loud noises outside the door. Scott looked out of the peephole and back at me. Grinning he said, "They here."

CHAPTER NINETEEN

YVETTE

"Let me clear the air. I'm in charge."

Scott called them Damper and Shelly B.

That's right...Shelly was a dude and he had to be the scariest thing I'd seen in a long time. Both of them stood over 6'4 which meant they completely towered over my much shorter frame. But Shelly B was the ugliest thing that only a mother could love and he was also gross.

Food smeared all over his white t-shirt.

Breath strong like garlic.

Just nasty.

Don't get me wrong, in terms of height I'm always the shortest thing in the room, but this was different and I was forced to feel a little intimidated. It was as if I were looking up at towers.

Shelly B, eating five slices of bread at a time walked up to me. Mouth full of food he said, "It's the only plan I got and if you ask me it's pretty damn good."

185

"I get all that but did you bother to think things through?" I yelled. "The way you trying to do this we gonna put them in a position where we're forcing them to show their hand. The thing is without the firepower we might come up on the losing end."

"You might not like my tactics but that's how I do things." Shelly B shrugged. "Hard, quick and fast. Besides, I thought you called us because your way wasn't working."

"My way always works, my nigga." I frowned. "Whether you know it or not. Don't get shit confused. Niggas have died for less." I nodded his way.

"We need to try a different approach, that's all I'm saying," he said.

"You talking about walking down the halls and blindly shooting into apartments. Now I'm not opposed to killing niggas but I don't do kids. It's not my thing now and it will never be."

He laughed. "I knew I shouldn't have answered the phone for that nigga," Shelly B said looking at Scott.

"You could always leave, my guy," Scott said. "It's really not a problem."

"Hold fast, Scott," I said extending my hand. "I want to know what this nigga meant by his comment."

"You see the difference between bitches and niggas is clear," Shelly B continued. "We do what's necessary while whores like—"

His sentence wasn't completed when Heavy slapped him so hard chunks of bread fell from his lips and bounced onto the floor. Shelly B made a move for his weapon but 88, Vance and Scott haulted him with guns aimed at his head.

I walked closer to Shelly B and grinned. Kicking the bread out my way I said, "I'm gonna be straight. I'm in a bind and I need your help, but you not 'bout to talk to me like you do that slut who gave birth to you. Now you may be put off by what's happening around here so let me clear the air. I'm IN CHARGE. And the moment you walked through that entrance that meant you became my property, free to do with as I please." I moved even closer. "And I please to have you do what the fuck I say or I'ma lay your fat ugly ass down. What's your preference?"

Frowning he looked at the guns and finally down at me. Slowly a smile etched across his face "Come on,

'Vette, I think you got shit the wrong way. I didn't mean it like that. I'm here because I fuck with you and the whole women's movement."

"That's why we're having this moment to clear things up. So that you see things my way. The only way." I paused. "I respect the wild side of you but wild animals can be put down." I paused. "Now...like I said, I don't do kids. So your plan won't work for me."

"Then what you wanna do?" Shelly B continued. "Because the reason you can't make it safely on that floor is because they must've hired help. You got the hallway and from the left and the right are other apartments. As you know #745 is basically in the middle. Since there is no entrance on the opposite side of the hallway we can only come down through the elevator or the stairway, which they have secured. Basically they see us coming before we can have a chance to react."

"Do we know who may be helping them?" I asked everyone.

Damper cleared his throat. "Not sure if this is correct or not, but one of my sources told me Wilson has some friends in that hallway who are working with them," Damper continued. "He's been feeding them your coke as payment and all they have to do is lookout of the peephole on a regular. If they see you or any of your people they've been instructed to shoot to kill."

My brows lowered. "Why didn't you tell me this shit the moment you stepped through my front door?" I frowned. "Bitch ass nigga in here wasting time."

He sighed. "Because I hear rumors constantly. No need to spread it around if it's not true."

I was so angry now I had a migraine. "You mean to tell me them niggas are in their peeling off my coke? Shot my best friend and snatched Carissa?" I asked no one in particular. I don't care who was inside or who they were with, once I got Carissa back safely then I was killing each one of them. With my bare hands if time permitted.

"I need somebody who knows a lot of phone numbers of the people in this building." I asked the room.

Dukes stepped up quietly. "I don't mean to interrupt but I know somebody."

I frowned. "Who?"

"She's locked in the supply closet." She paused. "But if you get her out she has almost every phone number for everyone in this building. Definitely the seventh floor."

I smiled. "Cool, 88 let Kisha out. And Vance, make sure you sit with her and verify who lives in those apartments."

"And then what?" Damper asked.

"Then we give a slight warning for them to get out of dodge before we light that floor up!

I walked into my room and into the bathroom to wipe my face when Heavy came inside behind me. "How you feeling, 'Vette?"

"I don't want to talk about calling you Thick earlier."

"I don't care. How do you feel?"

I laughed and shook my head. "What you think? Mercedes in the room passed out and bleeding. I think Carissa gave Ryan too much Benadryl for his peanut butter allergy so she can stare at him because he hasn't woken up since. And we're at war."

"That's not what I asked you, Yvette." He walked into the bathroom and looked at my reflection in the mirror. "I asked how are *you*. And what can I do? For *you*?"

I turned around and examined his eyes. I felt I could trust him but I wasn't sure. "Are you being real with me? About everything?"

"Why you keep asking me that?" He yelled.

"Maybe I don't believe you. Maybe I think you holding back."

"I wouldn't be here if I wasn't for you. I wouldn't be putting my life on the line if I didn't care. Now if you gotta ask me if I'm being honest then maybe you should let me go so I—"

"I'm not letting you go. As a matter of fact you aren't going anywhere."

He smiled. "You sure about that? Because every time I see your face it's like you hate me and—"

"I got a lot going on, Heavy." I looked down at the floor. "I'm not as pretty as my friends or as nice. All I have is my business and my courage. Most of the men I come in contact with want something from me and I need to know that you're different."

"The only way you can find that out is through time. You don't get to know someone fully overnight. Trusting is a process, Yvette. I'm willing to see it through if you are."

"You have to give me time too, Heavy. It's all I can say at the moment. But I'm not a damsel in distress and you can't save me either."

He looked away and back at me. "I know. And I'm willing to wait because you're worth it. All I ask is that you come to me before believing the world, Yvette. People don't want us to be together and I need the chance always to explain myself first. Okay?"

There was a knock at the door. "We're ready," Damper said opening it up without an invitation. "You want us to go now?"

Damn these niggas rude. Whatever happened to knocking and waiting to be invited in?

"Yeah. We verified who lives on that floor yet?"

He smiled. "Yep, old girl had everybody's number. Half of the people we didn't need to call because she knew who was home and who wasn't. She's in the kitchen eating the rest of the fried chicken. She said she knew you wouldn't mind since she helped you and all."

I rolled my eyes.

Greedy bitch.

"Aight...head out. And don't stop firing until the floor is covered with shells and bodies."

"We ain't come over here for nothing." He winked before walking out.

CHAPTER TWENTY

CARISSA

"If you gonna kill me be done with it already."

He raped me non-stop, only giving me time to pee and wash up before he did it again. All while a corpse lie in the bathroom. It was like he was getting off on it or something.

At first I couldn't look at him, wanting the moment to be over. But after awhile it became obvious that he wouldn't stop until he took everything from me.

He was reaching his fourth orgasm when finally he looked down into my eyes.

He grinned, got up and wiped his dick with the pillowcase mixed with sperm and blood that he used for the other sessions. "Let me guess. You're staring at me because you're in love now," He said laughing. "I know I have that effect on the ladies."

I remained silent, unwilling to play his games.

He chuckled again. "So you gonna play quiet? Because if you haven't guessed by now the more silent you are the more I find you attractive." He slipped on his baby blue boxers. "And you know what that means. We gonna have to go another round." He placed on his jeans.

"I don't care what you do anymore, Wilson. Just make it quick."

He shook his head. "Women always say that but I find they sing another song after a few hours. Most realize when it's all said and done they can't take the pain after all. As thin as you are, you won't be any different."

"You don't know me." I paused. "You know nothing about the things I've been through or seen. If you gonna kill me be done with it already and stop talking shit."

He laughed. The kind of laugh that told me he was enjoying this more than he should have. "I'm not gonna kill you, Carissa. That's not how I do things. Plus if you're gone who we gonna have for collateral?" He paused. "But I will give you an update. Your little friends were in for a rude awakening when they tried to walk down the yellow coke road an hour ago. They didn't realize how much clout we got and that them bricks in the kitchen can get a man to do anything. Including hold down the fort." He exhaled. "I'm not sure, but I think they hit one of your friends with a hot one."

My eyes widened. "You're lying!"

"Am I?"

I looked at him trying to determine if he was being honest. When I realized I read him wrong initially I frowned and turned away.

I was done talking. If he was going to play games I had no intentions on participating.

Just then the bedroom door opened and Rambler walked inside. "Kitty, called and—" She looked at me and her eyes widened. "Wait...you're in here raping her? Fuck wrong with you?"

She stared at my underwear on the floor, my nudity from the waist down and back at him.

"Even if I did get a shot of pussy ain't none of your business. Now what the fuck do you want?" He fastened his belt. "What Kitty say?"

Rambler's nostrils flared. "I'm not a part of this shit!" She pointed at me while looking at him. "I don't respect this at all."

"That's good because ain't nobody ask you for a three way, bitch!"

"I'm serious, Wilson. Ya'll came over here unwanted, took over and now you raping people? What's wrong with you?"

"Not people. Just one person," he said. "And she ain't fight too much. I think she likes it."

"This ain't no fucking game!"

"I'm warning you, Rambler. If you know what's good for you, you'd back out and go wait in the living room."

She placed her hands on her hips and walked closer to him. "And if I don't just what the fuck do you plan on doing? I'm not scared of you, Wilson. I never have been and I never —"

He punched her in the lips.

So hard blood flew from her mouth and onto the top of my toenail. When I say he opened the tissue of her face that's exactly what I mean. Instead of leaving it alone he bent down, grabbed her short gold hair and hit her in the face again, just as Grace walked inside.

"What the fuck you doing!" She looked like a madman. "Get the fuck off my friend!" She yelled as she hit him repeatedly on the back with her fists. "You're hurting her!"

When both of them started to jump him I was so hopeful that I would get out of this alive after all that I tried to wiggle out of my restraints. But he had the binding on my wrists around the bedframe so I had to wait.

As I watched the melee it was obvious that kidnapping me was not part of the girls' plan. But once again my hopes are short lived when he grabs Rambler's arm and bends it in the opposite direction, cracking it instantly.

Now broken it hung awkwardly to the left side.

Rambler's screeching cry sent chills up my spine.

"Fuck you do to her?" Grace yelled as she dropped on the floor next to her friend. "FUCK IS WRONG WITH YOU?" She yelled looking up at Wilson.

"I broke her fucking arm. What it look like? She better hope I don't put a bloody Bindi on her forehead next." He wiped the sweat from his brow along with the blood from the scratches on his face. "Now shut that bitch up before I break her neck next."

Grace slammed her hand over Rambler's mouth and rocked her silent.

WILSON

Corey approached Wilson as he walked out of the bedroom. Kliyo was sitting on the sofa, drinking a gallon of vodka from the bottle while Spotter was standing against the wall with a t-shirt wrapped around his nose.

The smell of the corpse bothered him the most but strangely enough Wilson didn't seem to mind it.

"Kitty keeps calling me," Corey said as he looked at Wilson's bloody scratched face. "What's going on back there? Why Rambler crying and Grace screaming?"

199

"Stop asking a million questions and tell me what she wanted!" Wilson yelled.

Corey gritted on him. "She said some nigga called her house earlier to confirm her son wasn't in the house. They must know we got niggas looking out the peephole for 'em."

"It don't matter, my man got a snow truck and he's digging it out now," Wilson said. "He should be out here in about three hours."

"Three hours and we'll all be dead," Spotter said, peeling himself off the wall. "There's no way they letting us get out of here with that coke. None. I wouldn't be surprised if they don't got niggas outside the door right now waiting for us. Everything about this shit was a suicide mission."

"You see, this is why I'm in charge and you're not," Wilson said slyly. "You have no vision. Don't get me wrong, you vicious with aiming and shooting but that's the extent of your skills. Why you think we took the bitch back there? What do you think the purpose of snatching her was?"

"Sounds to me like the purpose was for you to fuck her," Kliyo said looking down at the vodka bottle. "Not sure what part of the plan that is but — "

Wilson frowned. "You may wanna do your best to stay invisible, son." He pointed at him. "I haven't found out your *purpose here yet. And a man with no purpose is expendable."*

Kliyo sat back and took another sip.

Wilson focused back on Corey. "Now what did Kitty mean they wanted to see if her kid was home? Fuck type question is that?"

"I don't know but she said they were calling everybody on the floor. Asking the same shit…if people had kids."

Suddenly gunfire sounded out in the hallway. It was as if a thousand bullets were smashing into the doors and walls. Slugs crashing against surfaces and shells dropping on the floor were so abundant they almost couldn't hear each other.

"It's started, gentlemen," Wilson said. "Time to suit up and earn our keep."

CHAPTER TWENTY-ONE

CARISSA

"When you ask me have I ever been in love, bitch you don't know the half."

I could tell from the bullets crashing into the doors that my family was here, on this floor. I looked across the room at Grace who was still rocking Rambler, who looked like she was doing her best to not pass out due to the pain of her broken arm.

"Was it worth it?" I asked them as war went on outside of the apartment. They looked at me. "Was all of this fucking worth it?" I repeated. "Worth him?"

Grace wiped the tears running down her face. "Have you ever loved a man so much that when he's not around you don't know what to do? What to feel or what to think? I'm not talking about a few moments of the day, I mean every moment...every second...every breath...without him you're lost."

202

I laughed softly, but not really. "What kind of question is that?"

"You asked me if it was worth it. If doing all of this for Heavy made sense. And I'm asking you a question before I answer."

I sighed. "I wanted to be a translator when I was younger. Most people don't know that. I thought that if I was a translator and learned Korean I could travel and see the world. That didn't happen. Instead I met a man who ate, breathed and lived cocaine." I shook my head as Lavelle's face flashed in my mind briefly.

"He convinced me that he couldn't do the business thing without me and my life has been changed ever since," I continued. "So when you ask me have I ever been in love, bitch you don't know the half. I gave up a career and my life for mine and I have nothing to show for it but a dead child and a broken heart. Anyway, that nigga back at our crib not even feeling you. Your situation and mine are polar opposites."

She nodded. "You may be right. But before today, with that dead nigga in the bathroom, I've never been with another man sexually. Heavy was the love of my life and my daughter's father. I couldn't walk away.

No, I didn't get him but if he'll take me back, even now, I'll gladly be with him."

"And you thought this was the way to win him over, Grace?" I paused. "By taking over our Trap? Open your fucking eyes. You failed."

"This was never my plan. The only thing I wanted was to get his attention. My cousin went too far."

"But you killed a man, for what?"

"I wanted Heavy to know I was serious!" She yelled. "I tried talking to him before all of this. I stopped by his apartment to get some of my things but he wouldn't hear me. He wouldn't reason. So I thought I could get him to come here, if he was worried that Yvette would think he was trying to rob her."

"Did it work?" I rolled my eyes.

"What you think?"

I didn't want to fight with her anymore and the gunfire sounded louder, as if they were getting closer. "Can you please let me go?" I pleaded. "This isn't how you planned things happening and I can still talk to my friends. If you let me go I will convince them that it was not your fault." I paused. "But you got to take me up on my offer now."

204

PITBULLS IN A SKIRT

The gunfire ceased.

Suddenly there was a banging on the front door in the apartment and Grace rushed out of the bedroom and left the door open. I was relieved because they had been closing the door in the past. Not only was Quinton's corpse starting to stink bad but I couldn't hear what was going on in the living room.

With the door open I would know and get fresh air.

WILSON

THIRTY MINUTES LATER

Wilson hung next to the door with Kliyo, Corey, Spotter and Grace behind him. He took a deep breath and talked to the door. "I'm not gonna be able to do that, Kitty. Sorry baby girl. Wish I could help you."

"Please, Wilson, you gotta let me inside." Her voice was frantic and she sounded as if she were about to die. "They killed everyone in the apartment."

"So how did you escape?"

"I hid in the stairwell, on the 4th floor when they started asking questions. I knew something was up that's why I kept calling. And now I'm afraid they know I'm involved and will come for me next. Please, Wilson. Let me inside."

"Where they at? Now?"

"I don't know!" She yelled banging on the door. "Open the fucking door and stop playing around. I'm scared!"

"I said no. I smell a trap and until I can be sure what's good nobody coming in this house."

"It's not a set up please let me — " Kitty's sentence was cut short by a single gunshot in the hallway, on the other side of the door. Everybody but Kliyo went for their weapons and aimed at the door despite it being shut.

"Kitty!" Wilson screamed. "You still out there?" When she didn't answer Wilson grew annoyed. "KITTY, WHERE THE FUCK YOU AT?"

What seemed like forever stood in place of an answer until suddenly Yvette's voice boomed from the other side. "She's dead, Wilson...you see why all of this has to stop?

Now." Yvette said calmly. "She's dead and from the way I see things this is kind of your fault."

Wilson looked back at Spotter and Corey who paced the floor. Focusing back on the door he said, "Ain't no Wilson in here. You got the wrong address."

Yvette laughed. "You see, that's a lie too. I got someone with me who knows that voice. No more games. Let's get to know each other while we still can."

He frowned. "So what now, 'Vette? You think you in charge or something?"

"Nah, my nigga. That's all you. You got the power."

"How come it don't feel like it?" He continued talking to the door.

"Because I'm gonna assist you in a decision so you'll go the right way," Yvette continued. "Now let me tell you what's happening." Yvette was so calm it was as if she was talking to a child she loved, one who misbehaved and whose actions she was trying to correct. "Outside of this door there are many men. And all of these men, including me, have a few intentions. And they are to come into that apartment. Get our friend and that dog food."

Wilson laughed although it was apparent he was afraid. He didn't sound as confident as he did when he was raping Carissa.

What a difference an army made.

"And just how do you plan on doing that? This door is reinforced metal with a bar over it. You and your crew saw to that remember?"

"The how is not your problem, my nigga," 88 added. "What you should be focusing on is the when. Ask yourself when we coming inside."

Wilson moved closer to the door and looked out of the peephole. From his vantage point he could see Yvette and too many men to count. "Don't forget...I have your friend," Wilson threatened. "You try anything stupid and she will –"

"Wilson, listen to me," Yvette said cutting him off. "If you hurt a hair on her head, I'm talking her scalp, her lashes or her brows, the pain I have in store for you will be unimaginable. Wilson, have you ever-experienced pain so harsh that you can't breathe? I'm talking torture so bad the simple act of grabbing oxygen only enhances the pain? Do yourself a favor, stop threatening my friend."

Wilson swallowed. "Listen, bitch – "

PITBULLS IN A SKIRT

"No you fucking listen! You kidnapped my friend and I want you to open this door now!" Yvette's voice grew angrier, almost psychotic. "But you should know I'm coming in regardless, Wilson. And if I come in without an invitation you gonna have a problem on your hands you not equipped to deal with. So open the door, Wilson. You don't have any business being in there. You and I both know it. Be smart."

Wilson looked back at his friends whose eyes told him that they would be of no help. "I'm sorry, Yvette, but the answer is no."

"I wish you hadn't said that." Yvette paused. "Kick the mothafucka in!" She told Scott and Vance who slammed the battering ram into the door, denting it instantly.

CHAPTER TWENTY-TWO

WILSON

"If they come in this mothafucka we all dead!

*T*he constant banging at the door and it folding slightly let everyone inside know that it would be caving in at any moment.

Wilson paced the floor as Kliyo, Corey, Spotter and Grace looked at him. Even Rambler sat in the doorway of the bedroom, arm still throbbing due to being broken to see what was happening. The only positive Rambler experienced was that when she left it in place, it didn't hurt as much as when she tried to move it.

Grace walked up to Wilson and took a deep breath. "What you gonna do, cuz? 'Cause we on some next war shit right now."

Wilson rubbed his throbbing temples, with the hand that still held the gun. "I need everyone to be quiet for just one fuckin' minute! If you not helping me think just shut the fuck up!"

Folks gave him his peace but the banging on the door didn't cease and that last blow made them think for certain it would be caving in at any moment. People were antsy and very uncomfortable.

But it was Grace who was unable to handle waiting on an answer from him anymore so she moved closer. "What we gonna do, Wilson? You had long enough to think already!"

"I DON'T KNOW WHAT THE FUCK TO DO!" He yelled in her face, spit flying from his mouth and landing against her nose. "If they come in this mothafucka we all dead! Know that shit while you busy asking questions like I'm the only one they gunning for." He walked a few feet away and flopped on the sofa.

BANG. BANG. BANG. BANG.

"They want the girl," Kliyo said softly. "And the coke. Just give them to 'em."

"Never. If you think I'm letting that bitch go then you got another thing coming. And I thought I told you to keep quiet?" Wilson frowned. "Why you even talking to me, nigga? You don't know me."

Kliyo walked to the wall and leaned against it. "This shit ain't ending too well. I can already tell."

"Well I'm gonna say something," Spotter said. "Why shouldn't we give her to them and see if we can negotiate?"

"Let me tell you how it'll go down if we do. We open the door, and say, 'Here she is. Other than Wilson fucking her a few times she's as good as new,'" he said sarcastically. "Do you know what they'll do? Huh? Shoot us in the fucking faces! That's what they'll do." He took a deep breath. "Listen, I know ya'll niggas scared but we give them bitches that girl then we need to call our mothers and say goodbye. She's the only thing keeping us alive for the moment." Wilson schooled. "

"If we don't do anything we'll die anyway, Wilson." Spotter continued before walking to the window. "You made a mistake by coming here, man. Shit happens. Maybe we can still get out of this in some fashion."

"Or we could jump." Corey suggested as he pulled the blinds string down and looked outside of the window. "The snow is high and it'll act like a cushion."

"Act like a cushion," Wilson repeated sarcastically. "What the fuck? We too high up for anything to be *cushiony."* Wilson *paused. "If the fall doesn't break our necks the ice cold will kill us. Sit the fuck down, nigga."*

"So I ask again, what's the plan?" Corey yelled. "Because we gotta do something and fast."

After hearing them go over the plan Rambler eased inside of the room and closed the door with her foot. She walked up to Carissa and sat on the edge of the bed. "What's going on out there?" Carissa asked with wide eyes. "They started whispering and I couldn't hear. And why you close the door?"

Rambler took a deep breath, also doing her best not to move her arm. "Are you religious?"

Carissa's eyes widened. "Fuck does that mean?"

"Are you a religious person? Do you believe in God?"

Carissa looked around the room and back at her. "I've been raped over ten times today. My pussy throbs and my waist hurts from the pressure he put on it from digging into my bones with his thumbs. The last thing I need right now is the games." Carissa scooted toward the edge of the bed. "Now what the fuck is going on out there in the living room?"

Rambler took a deep breath. "Wilson and them gonna hurt you."

Carissa shrugged. "They hurt me already. What do I give a fuck?"

"I'm not talking about that kind of pain, Carissa. I'm talking about the kind that never dies." She paused. "They thinking about torturing you so your friends will back away from the door."

Carissa looked at the closed bedroom door and sighed. "But...my friends still gonna come in."

"I don't think they give a fuck." Rambler swallowed. "It's the only thing they can think of at the moment. So if you – "

"Let me out of this." Carissa raised her arms. "Please! That way I can at least fight for my life."

"I have one hand, Carissa. I mean look at me." Rambler *gazed down at her arm, which she tied closely to her body to prevent it from moving, causing excruciating pain. "My arm is broken." She paused. "I'm of no use to you."*

Tears rolled down her face. "I can't believe all of this is happening. It's like I'm in a nightmare."

"You ARE in a nightmare," Rambler said.

The bedroom door came flying open and Wilson rushed inside.

Rambler moved out their way.

Corey untied the bind from the bed that held Carissa and Wilson grabbed her by her hair and dragged her through the open bedroom door. The sound of Yvette and her crew trying to get inside the Trap was now so loud it was deafening. Once at the door Wilson tossed her down, rushed to the kitchen and grabbed the biggest knife he could find.

He moved quickly for Carissa and she squirmed again until he stole her in the nose, forcing her still. "YVETTE, I GOT YOUR FRIEND RIGHT HERE!" He yelled. "DO YOU HEAR ME? I'M LOOKING AT YOUR FUCKING FRIEND!"

Suddenly the noise stopped.

"Carissa," Yvette said softly. "You there?"

Blood streamed out of Carissa's nose from where Wilson hit her and into her mouth. With a trembling voice full of fear she said, "Yes...I'm here." She paused. "Are you okay?" Yvette asked Carissa.

"Not even close, 'Vette. I'm...I'm sorry." Carissa swallowed the blood that filled her mouth. "I'm sorry for leaving and if Mercedes is with you, tell her I'm sorry too."

"Don't worry about all that, Carissa, you gonna be alright," Yvette said. "I'm gonna get you out of there."

"Not this time, 'Vette," Carissa cried. "Not this — "

Wilson kicked Carissa in the gut forcing her quiet. "I hate to break this party up but we have something to discuss," Wilson said to the door. "I have what you want and you have what I want, Yvette."

"And what the fuck is that?" Yvette asked. "Because I can't wait to get my hands on you, nigga!" She kicked the door. "Do you hear me? I'M GONNA FUCKING KILL YOU!"

Wilson laughed. "I wanna see if you'll still feel that way after what I'm about to do next."

CHAPTER TWENTY-THREE

YVETTE

"Okay, Wilson. You got it this time."

Me, Heavy and 88 stood outside the Trap door. Scott and Vance were holding the battering ram, which was making some headway.

Until Wilson made threats.

We suddenly were paused for the moment.

"What you talking about, Wilson?" I asked.

"Do you love your friend?" Wilson continued. "I mean do you really care about her? Like you claim to do?"

"You better stop fucking around!" I yelled taking a fist to the door. My skin so hot when I looked down at my arm it was strawberry red. "You making shit worse than ever for yourself. Whether you realize it or not, we getting in this apartment!"

"I asked a fuckin' question." Wilson said forcefully. "Do you love her or not?"

For some reason I thought about Mercedes who was sleeping in the apartment, recovering from a bullet wound. For a second I took in how angry she was when we left the shootout earlier and I realized why her rage went deeper. As much as she and Carissa fought they loved each other and I think I knew why.

It wasn't about the grandchild they shared.

I think it was because when I was out in the trenches, during the Emerald City days, they were forced to grow closer.

It was me who held shit down and kept the soldiers in line.

It was me who made sure the product entered the city and was distributed properly.

I always knew my place in the organization because Thick taught me well but all they had was each other. And if we lost Carissa, like we did Kenyetta, it would be devastating for Mercedes.

And for me.

I took a deep breath and placed one hand on the dented Trap door. "I'm listening."

"That's better," Wilson said. "What you gonna do is back away from this fucking door and then you gonna go down the hallway and off this floor. And you gonna do it now."

"Why the fuck would I do—"

Suddenly I heard Carissa's screeching cry and felt my blood boil. "KICK THIS FUCKING DOOR IN!" I yelled to Scott and Vance. "DO IT NOW!"

"YOU BETTER NOT!" Wilson yelled. "You not gonna kick shit in and I'm gonna tell you why." He paused. "Your friend is screaming because I just ran a kitchen blade down her arm. I want you to know that the next one is going across her throat and then wrists. Now back away from the fucking door or stand by while I kill this whore! Now!"

"FUCK!" I yelled as I paced the area in front of me. I wanted this nigga's blood so bad I felt like a vamp.

"We gotta do it, Yvette," 88 whispered to me. "We gotta leave because he got the upper hand right now and we need to go back to the drawing board." He paused and moved closer to her. "I'm not willing to take a chance with Carissa's life and I know Mercedes wouldn't either. I'm speaking for my girl right now, 'Vette. Let's go."

I turned around and looked at my team before focusing on the door. "Okay, Wilson. You got it this time."

"I can't here you," He laughed.

"I said you got it, nigga!" I yelled.

"I know I do." He paused. "But to be sure I'm sending Kliyo out in five minutes. If he sees any one of you I'm killing this Indian looking bitch dead. After that who gives a fuck what happens to us. We all gonna die eventually."

"Aight, Wilson!" I looked at my people. "Let's go." Slowly we crept away from the door.

Real slowly.

WILSON

PITBULLS IN A SKIRT

Wilson looked out of the peephole and smiled when he saw everyone dispersed. He released the hold he had on Carissa's hair and looked back at his crew. "They gone." He looked down at Carissa and her bloody arm. "They fucking gone!" He said excitedly as if he was really winning. When he heard Carissa weeping he said, "Somebody take her in the fucking room. She's ruining my good mood."

Spotter and Corey rushed toward Carissa and each of them grabbed an arm. "You gonna die, nigga" Carissa yelled spitting blood on the floor. "Do you hear me, you gonna die!"

"Fuck you, bitch!" Wilson laughed. When Carissa was secured back in the bedroom and the door was closed, Corey and Spotter walked back into the living room. "Now do you believe me?" Wilson asked them. "Now do you — "

"If you think shit is ending like this you way outta your league, Wilson," Corey said cutting him off. "Trust me when I say this shit just getting started."

"All I know is this...one minute they were crashing through the door and the next they ain't. Now I know it's not the solution to our problem but it's a start."

"We need to be thinking on a plan to get out of here," Spotter said. "I mean out the building. It's not snowing no more but it won't be long before they plow and their soldiers come through on some hunt shit."

Wilson walked toward Kliyo who was sitting on the sofa looking up at him. "What?" He said with a major attitude. "Why you in my face all of a sudden? I thought I didn't know you."

"Get up, nigga," Wilson said waving his hand. "You been running your mouth non stop and now its time to earn your keep." When he didn't move Wilson got angrier. "I said get the fuck up before I punch you in the teeth!"

Kliyo's eyes widened but he remained seated. "What you want me to do? I ain't got no fucking gun."

"You don't need one. What you gonna do is go out in the hallway and make sure they're gone," he instructed. "When you finish you gonna come back and let me know. It's simple. Now move."

Kliyo rose slowly. "I can't go out there, they think I'm with ya'll now. Because of all the lies you made me tell them on the phone. That means if they haven't gone the first thing they gonna do is shoot me in the face. Fuck that shit. I'm staying right here."

"You getting shot in the face is not my problem or concern. Truth is I could care less. Should've never let them bitches in here." He laughed.

"But it's hot out there right now, man." Kliyo pleaded. "Come on, don't make me do this. If I walk into the hallway I'm basically committing suicide."

Wilson placed the cool barrel of his gun against Kliyo's temple. "Nigga, it's about to get hotter in here too. Now take your bitch ass out in the hallway and see if they're gone. I'm not 'bout to ask you again."

"Fuck! This wrong as shit, man." Kliyo moped to the door so slowly it was as if he was moving backwards. Finally with a yank and a shove he pushed the dented door open. He looked out and looked back at Wilson. "It's clear."

"Nigga…walk all the way out!" Wilson yelled. "Stupid ass mothafucka!"

Mad at the world, Kliyo walked into the hallway, the door slamming behind him. It smelled of gunpowder like a firework session on the fourth of July. Doors to the left of the apartment were kicked in and hanging out.

Gun shells were everywhere.

Dead bodies of those who originally tried to shoot at Yvette and Mercedes were lying in the apartments.

It took only a moment for him to discern the obvious. It was empty, true enough, but there was one person waiting.

Quietly.

Yvette.

He was about to run until she said, "Don't be afraid. I got a message for you that I want you to pass on."

"Yee...yessss," he said, his voice trembling.

"Tell Wilson when its time for me to kill ya'll niggas, I kissed the bullet that belongs to him. He's gonna die by my hand personally...believe that." She walked away and out of sight.

CHAPTER TWENTY-FOUR

HEAVY

"That's gonna be impossible considering the gunplay taking place around here."

*H*eavy paced the living room floor trying to figure out how he tied into all of this mess. His mind was racing but when he looked over at Yvette she seemed extra strong and he started falling for her even more. As much as everything was coming down on her, she seemed unmoved.

He never met a woman like that before and if she left him he doubted he'd ever would again.

Heavy placed a hand on her shoulder. "'Vette, you okay?"

She looked up at him and gave him a half smile. "Don't...don't worry about me in that way. I'm not helpless, Heavy. I told you that already."

He removed his hand and took a deep breath. "I know, bae. But that's gonna be impossible considering the gunplay taking place around here."

225

"Still, I don't need that type of attention right now."

She walked up to Shelly B, Vance, Damper, Scott and 88 with Heavy following. "They have us where they want us for the moment. I'm gonna need more men who can't get in this building until this snow melts. It's not coming down anymore but – "

Dukes, Rocky and Kisha came out into the living room cautiously. "Go back in there with Mercedes," Yvette told them. "I don't want your eyes coming off of her until she's out of that bed." Kisha immediately turned around with an attitude and walked back into the bedroom.

"We have an idea," Rocky said to Yvette. "To help you get them out of the apartment."

Yvette turned toward them. "And what is that?"

"They can't stay in the Trap. I'm talking about Wilson and them." Rocky said. "They know you're gunning for them so they'll need to hide before the snow gets plowed. That way they'll get a ride out maybe with your coke and friend."

"And?" Yvette shrugged. "Get to the point quicker."

"That's where me and Dukes come in. We can be their escape plan."

Yvette grinned. "I'm listening."

WILSON

Wilson sipped on a whiskey while looking out of the window. He closed the blind and sat on the sofa. "They should be coming to get us in any minute. I just got off the phone with my cousin. All we have to do is —"

"Nigga, ain't nobody coming to save us!" Spotter yelled. "Either we get out of this bitch on our own or we don't! But please stop feeding us fairy tales."

Wilson looked up at him, put the glass on the floor. "You gotta have a better attitude about this shit. It's because of me you still breathing."

Spotter wiped his hand down his face. "I'm walking out of here and I'm walking out now."

"Good, go ahead," Wilson, laughed. "Because I'm gonna wait on —"

"Have you ever stopped to realize that just like we waiting on our ride, that Yvette and 'em are waiting on their cavalry too?" Corey continued. "I wonder which crew will get here first. Your weed-head cousin and his fat bitch, or the forty seven niggas C and them bitches bringing."

Wilson's jaw twitched. "Since you so smart what do you think we should do?"

"Now he listens," Corey responded. "This is my idea...we take the coke and find somebody's apartment in this building and hide out."

Wilson stood up slowly and scratched his head. "That's a good idea...a real good one." He paused. "But when the forty seven niggas you talking about get here, what's to stop them from kicking in all 98 doors in this building until they find us?"

Corey moved closer. "You thinking too small, Wilson. You gotta think bigger. Even if they spread out they not getting in these doors at the same time. If we get into another apartment we can wait them out and meet your cousin and his bitch. We jump in his truck and we'll be home free. Coke and all."

Wilson nodded and pointed at him. "Yeah...so all we gotta do is grab an apartment on the ground floor. So we'll be closer to an exit."

"No...they'll check their first but guess where they won't think we're dumb enough to hide...on this floor right here."

Wilson smiled. "Let me find out you're not as stupid as I thought." He rubbed his hands together. "So this is what we gonna do, we're gonna go find an apartment that's – "

"Bitch, I'm not fucking around with you! Get out of my apartment!" They heard a woman yell down the other side of the hall, outside of the Trap house. It was away from the stairwell. Yvette and her crew didn't have to kick in those doors because they were on the opposite side of apartment #745.

Wilson grabbed his hammer and moved to the door before looking out the peephole. "I can't see them but I think they on the other side of us." He looked back at his men. "I'm about to find out." He paused. "Come with me, Spotter. Corey you stay and watch the bitch." He pointed at him. "I want to make sure the coast is clear before we take her out of here."

Kliyo stood up. "What about me?"

Wilson smiled at him and said, "Oh yeah…you can hold this…" He shot him in the stomach.

RAMBLER

Carissa looked up at Rambler after hearing the gunshot from Wilson shooting Kliyo, fearing the worst had yet to happen. Grace was in the corner on the phone and Quinton's corpse stunk up the room even more.

"Did you hear that gunshot?" Carissa asked them. "It's about to happen. They gonna kill me. Please let me out."

"Like I keep telling you I can't do shit," Rambler said. "I might have been involved in the original plan but now it's not me…you gotta talk to her." She pointed to Grace.

Grace got off of the call and walked toward them. Looking at Rambler she said, "That was Heavy. He said he's gonna get us out of here once things calm down and Yvette's men get here."

Rambler frowned. "Now why would he do that? This is mostly our fault. If anything he's gonna snatch us and kill us to prove himself to her."

"He'll do it," Grace frowned. "He'll save us. Plus he knows that I never meant for any of this to happen. Trust me, in all of my life he's never let me down. Even if he's mad at me."

Rambler sighed. "Open your fuckin eyes, bitch! He's letting you down now! You did all of this for him and don't have nothing to show for it."

"That's your view of things Rambler, please don't ask me to make them mine."

CHAPTER TWENTY-FIVE

WILSON

"Do you know about what's been going
on in this building? With the bullets
flying?"

A fter some quick investigation on their part, Wilson
*and Spotter discovered where the commotion was
coming from as they walked into the hallway. Wilson focused
on Dukes and Rocky fighting outside of their apartment and
tilted his head. He'd seen them around Marjorie but didn't
have any real conversation for them either which way.*

But now he was interested.

*Wilson immediately looked at Spotter and smiled.
"We're up," he whispered. "Let's make this situation work
for us. Quick before Yvette and them come back."*

*The two men rushed up to the women before they could
go back inside of their apartment. Instead of scaring them to
death by putting a weapon to their heads, Wilson hid his gun
in his jeans, placed his palms in the air and decided to play
the mediator. "Now, now, ladies, what's this about?" Every*

232

other second he'd look down the opposite end of the hallway to be sure Yvette and her crew wasn't creeping.

For now he was safe.

Him being cautious was the main reason they didn't want to bring Carissa with them. Had they brought her with them and it was an ambush Yvette would snatch Carissa and get what she came for.

Killing him next.

He had to be smart.

"Mind your fucking business, "Dukes yelled at Wilson. "This don't have nothing to do with you so we'd appreciate if you would just stay the fuck out of it."

"I know it ain't my business, mami, I know...just wanting to help that's all," Wilson said. "Plus I don't want to fight with you. You look like you would kick my ass."

"And like my friend said we got this," Rocky yelled. "We having a little disagreement that's all." She continued crossing her arms across her white t-shirt. She changed out of her bloodied scrubs so Wilson wouldn't be more suspicious.

Wilson's jaw twitched because what he wanted to do was punch both of them in the face but he was playing the long con game and needed to take his time.

For the moment anyway.

"We're not the enemy, beautiful," Spotter said, figuring he could lend some help since Wilson was coming up short. "We're here to – "

"Nigga, get the fuck up out my face!" Dukes yelled so loud she spit on his upper lip. "Why are ya'll still here anyway? Damn! It's fucking stupid! Go away and worry about your own business, faggies!"

Rocky looked at Dukes through the corner of her eye. The goal was to not give in so easily so that they wouldn't suspect a set up but Dukes was acting like she was going for the Oscar. It was one thing to make them thing the argument was genuine and a whole different matter to be so difficult that they walked off or shot them in the forehead.

"Listen, can we talk in the apartment 'bout this?" Wilson asked tired of faking it. His patience had run thin and there was no longer a smile on his face. "I hate doing things like this in the hallway."

Any other time Rocky would've sent him on his way but now was not the time to play hard to get. Rolling her eyes she said, "I guess so." She opened the door wider and both men walked inside, ahead of her and Dukes.

"Bitch, you was going too far," Rocky whispered to Dukes, out of earshot of the fellas.

Dukes rolled her eyes. "They in here aren't they? So it worked."

Rocky closed the door and the moment she did Wilson shot Dukes in the stomach. "OH MY GOD WHY DID YOU DO THAT?" Rocky screamed. "WHY DID YOU SHOOT MY FRIEND?"

"I hate to be called a faggy." Wilson rushed toward her and slapped her in the face to calm her down. "Look at me..."

But she wasn't looking at him. Instead she was hysterical as she looked down at her friend who was holding her stomach, too shocked to speak.

"Why did you do that?" Rocky continued to cry. "Why did you shoot her?"

"I just told you." Wilson grabbed a hold of her face and looked into her eyes. "Now look at me...is...this...a...set...up? Did Yvette and them have you come into the hallway with this shit? 'Cause I find it mighty convenient you know what I'm saying? Do you know about what's been going on in this building? With the bullets

flying on this floor and shit? You saw the carnage out there?"

"Nigga, this is Marjorie Gardens." She said through clenched teeth. "Bullets always fly around here."

"Don't be smart, bitch." He slapped her again. "Are you setting me up? Answer me!"

Rocky was scared into another religion but she knew if she didn't get herself together she would be on the floor next to her friend, who died seconds earlier. Slowly Rocky looked at him and glared. "No…this ain't no set up. Now what you want from me?"

He backed up a little and tilted his head sideways. "Oh you mad now? You 'bout to be hard and shit and defend your friend's death?" He pointed at Dukes' body. "I have no problem shooting you too. 'Cause I still don't trust the situation."

Although he threatened her actually he did have a problem with murdering her. He let off too many rounds and was dry. He had one more bullet left in his gun and needed it in case he had to hit one of Yvette's men.

"You killed my friend," she said through clenched teeth. "Why wouldn't I be mad? Now what do you want with me? I keep asking and you not saying nothing."

PITBULLS IN A SKIRT

He liked her roar. She wasn't scared and that was attractive considering the situation. "Actually I'm surprised you so upset about shawty. The way you were acting a minute ago in the hallway I would think I did you a favor. By shooting your friend and all." He shrugged again. "But hey...maybe I made a mistake. My bad." He looked back at Spotter. "Check the crib and make sure nobody else is in here."

"On it," Spotter said.

Wilson grabbed her hand and walked over to the sofa. He sat down and pulled her to the seated position also. "Now, I want you to tell me about yourself. Starting with your name."

"Rocky..."

"So what does Rocky do around here? Come on...tell me more."

Rocky was so angry she could spit in his face. Her rage was the main reason her grandmother nicknamed her Rocky. Whenever she got upset unlike a lot of people in her family she couldn't hold her composure and preferred to box her way out of a situation instead. While she looked at him she wanted to steal him in the jaw but thought better of it.

"Ain't nothing to know about me." She said rolling her eyes. "I'm here and I'll die soon."

"You can die even sooner if you don't be a little kinder." He paused. "Now I know you mad about shawty but try not to get shot over spilled blood okay?"

Rocky nodded.

"It's empty, man," Spotter said coming back into the living room. "Looks like this is the place to be." He rubbed his hands together.

Wilson stood up and grinned. "Okay, go get Carissa and the work and bring them back." He looked at Rocky and sighed. "I hope you don't mind if we hang around here for a little while. Even if you do, well, nobody gives a fuck."

"I'll be right back," Spotter said as he moved for the door in a hurry. "Make sure you let me back in when I knock."

"I got you." Wilson winked at him as he walked out.

Wilson looked her up and down. "I been meaning to ask from the time I saw you last summer at the cookout 'Vette and them threw. You got a man, beautiful? Because somebody with a personality like yours could be on my arm if she acted right."

"Yeah...I'm taken."

He sat down and leaned back into the sofa. "Word...tell me about this nigga."

Rocky had zero time for the games but had to keep herself together. "He ain't really my type but I gave it a try," she lied. "It's still early so I'll see where it goes." She looked at her friend and looked away again, trying her best not to be emotional. When she agreed to help Yvette and her team being humiliated and losing her friend was not part of the plan.

Only if she could turn back time.

"So where you meet him at? Your man. Please don't tell me you fuckin' a nigga from Marjorie. Ain't none of the dudes 'round here about shit. Present company included." He winked before laughing at his own joke.

"I did meet him from around here...he...he..." Her voice trailed off and a tear crept down her cheek for Dukes' sake. Feeling weak, she swatted it away. "Gotta see how it goes after a little time I guess."

He nodded. "I get that...but if things don't work out I'd like to put my bid in now. I got shit with me but for a sexy red head like yourself, I might be willing to change. That is if you don't mind getting to know a nigga."

"Shoot your shot, playa-playa." She said under her breath, having no intentions on pursuing the creep.

"That I will do." He grinned. "I like you, Red Head. And I prefer to keep women close to me that I like." There was a knock at the door and he grabbed her by the arm and snatched her toward it like a rag doll. Once there he glanced out the peephole. Looking outside he only saw Spotter. "Where the bitch and the dope?" He yelled at the door.

"They won't let me in, Wilson!" Spotter said angrily.

"Fuck! You gotta come out here and tell them to let me in."

Wilson felt something was off and took a moment to play the moves in his head. Either his cousin Grace decided to keep the dope and the girl for herself or Spotter was lying. The thing was he knew Spotter long enough to know he always had his back. Corey on the other hand was too green over Grace to see things his way and of course his cousin was fifty-fifty.

He also realized that if Grace was betraying him, there was no way he could let her stay in that Trap with both rewards by herself. If he was gonna die for something he was gonna die for a price.

So he opened the door.

GRACE

Rambler and Carissa sat on the living room sofa while Corey and Grace paced the floor. "Something is wrong, I can feel it," Grace said eyes moving wildly around the Trap house. "This is about to blow up in our faces."

"I know...I knew I couldn't trust that nigga...he gonna leave us with this shit," Corey said. "When Yvette and them come back I'm gonna be left with my dick in my hands."

"It's gonna be a bloody dick if she kicks that door in," Grace said.

When there was a knock at the door Corey moved toward it, relieved Wilson hadn't let them down. He looked out the peephole and back at them with a smile. "He came back. Guess he found a place for the stash after all."

"Wait, don't open the door," Grace yelled. "Let me make sure shit is good first."

"Bitch, you must be crazy. We gotta get out of here!" He turned to open the door when suddenly he felt a piercing slash in his lower back. When he looked over his shoulder he saw that Grace had stabbed him. "What...what is wrong with you?" With wide eyes he asked, "Why you do that?"

He dropped to the floor and she kicked him out of the way and looked out of the peephole. Wilson was by himself but something didn't add up. "Why you looking all crazy out there?" Grace asked. "You okay, cuz?"

"Open the door, man," he said under his breath. "I found a place for us. But Spotter said you wouldn't let us back in."

"I will...but is everything cool? Because I got a bad feeling. You're not your usual upbeat self."

"Yes I'm fine!" He took a fist to the door. "Now stop fucking around and open up! I need to help move the coke out before Yvette and them come back."

Grace looked back at Rambler and Carissa. "I'm gonna have to pass on this shit," she said to Rambler. "My instincts telling me not to make any moves."

"But what if he's telling the truth?" Rambler whispered. "We can't be in here forever. You know that. And my arm is killing me."

"I can't explain it but I can feel something is off, Rambler," She looked out of the peephole again. "Sorry, cousin, I'm not gonna be able to open the door. I'll get up with you though."

Wilson's jaw twitched and she felt she made the right decision. "So you gonna leave your own flesh and blood out here to die?"

"Is that what you call it? You slapped me. You humiliated me and now you call me your cousin?

"Bitch, stop fucking playing before I — "

His sentence was forever silenced when Yvette, using the bullet she kissed, shot him in the temple. With Wilson dead she came into view of the peephole with Heavy and 88 at her side. "You're a smart girl, Grace," Yvette said calmly through the door. "I always knew that about you."

Carissa tried to hide her smile although it was difficult. Her girl came back for her. But Kenyetta's death taught her that she could not claim the glory until she was home safe and in her bed sleep.

Grace, on the other hand, tried not to piss on herself feeling as if her life was coming to a tragic end. "Oh...yeah? How do you know I'm so smart?"

"Because you picked a real nigga when you chose Heavy. In that way I guess we have a lot in common. Which is why I'm giving you an opportunity to come out on your own. To give up my friend and my product. You gonna do that for me, Grace? Or you gonna make things harder?"

"I can't, Yvette. If I'm gonna die I guess I gotta kill your friend and myself."

"You don't really mean that, Grace. You already see where threatening my friend has gotten folks. DEAD. Come out now and open this door. Don't share Wilson and Spotter's fate."

"I can't do that," she grinned. "I'm so sorry."

YVETTE

I was exhausted and I wanted this to be over. In my mind, when this night went down I saw one scenario happening and I was trying to avoid it.

It would be my final sacrifice.

"Let us knock this door down," Vance said as he and Scott held the Battering Ram. "No sense in waiting when we're almost there. Whatever's gonna happen it has to happen now."

Heavy looked at me and said, "Baby, he's right. Let's not wait. I love you. And she may have been my child's mother but whatever you decide I'm supporting."

I smiled and looked up at him. "I love you too, Heavy. I know I didn't say it because I was afraid to express myself but I want you to know now."

"Yvette, we don't have time for all this," 88 whispered. "Let's bring your girl home."

I looked back at him, at Heavy and then the door. "Grace, open the door. This my last time asking."

Grace giggled. "And if I don't what's gonna happen?

"Either open the door or I'ma put a bullet in this nigga's head." I said referring to Heavy.

Heavy's eyes widened as 88 walked up behind him and pressed a gun to the back of his scalp. Shelly B on the other hand relieved Heavy's weapon quickly from him with a smile on his face since the tables were now turned.

"Bae, why you doing this?" Heavy asked with wide eyes. "I'm on your side."

"I know you are, Heavy, but my friend is in that apartment and I need her safe," I told him. "If I gotta kill you than so be it. Call it taking one for the team."

GRACE

Grace farted as she saw the gun being pressed against Heavy's head from the peephole. She stumbled backwards and looked at Rambler. "What's going on out there?" Rambler asked, trying desperately not to move her arm. "Are they gonna leave?"

"She's threatening to shoot Heavy," Grace said. "She's gonna...she's gonna..."

"Just open the door, Grace," Rambler begged. "This shit is over. Please don't make them kick it in. It'll just be worse."

Before she could give a response Yvette and her team was banging at the door again with the battering ram. It was all over. She could either give up with class or have it be done the hard way.

Either way she lost.

At that moment she thought about how the day started, when Heavy said he didn't want her. Now she felt stupid and more than anything she realized it wasn't worth it.

So Grace stood up straight, took a deep breath, kicked Corey's body further away and opened the door.

Now she was facing the love of her life and the woman who took him from her. "I'm done fighting. You won, Yvette."

"I always do," Yvette said.

Since the door was opened 88 rushed inside and picked Carissa up off the sofa, while Grace continued to look at Yvette and Heavy. Shelly B now had a gun pressed to the back of Heavy's head.

"So you left me for her," Grace said. "A woman who's threatening to have you shot. You call that love?"

Heavy remained silent and looked away.

"So let me guess, after all of this you still gonna be with him." Grace asked Yvette.

Yvette smiled. "That's where me and you differ. When it comes to my friends I don't fuck around." She looked back at Shelly B. "Aye, yo, drop this nigga."

With that Shelly B shot Heavy in the back of the head and his body flopped as Yvette's eyes remained on Grace. Like he never mattered. "You see that shit?" Yvette pointed down at him. "Consider that the fall from Grace. And you don't have nobody to blame but yourself."

"You...you killed him!" Grace cried covering her mouth. She went ballistic with wide eyes and quick breaths. "I thought you cared about him!"

Yvette walked closer to Grace and sighed. "I DID care about him...I even loved him ...but where you got me fucked up is when you took my friend. When it comes to her or

248

PITBULLS IN A SKIRT

Mercedes, I don't play. Now you know." She turned around and walked out but not before saying, "Kill everybody in that Trap."

POW! POW! POW!

EPILOGUE

SIX MONTHS LATER

Dipped in a black Versace jumpsuit, Yvette stood on her veranda and looked at the small lake she built on her private property in Virginia. She hadn't owned it long but there was something about the way the water sloshed against the rocks quietly that put her at ease. She had just taken another sip of wine when Mercedes and Carissa stepped out to join her, standing on opposite sides of her small frame.

Earlier they had lunch but something felt off and she needed fresh air.

She looked back at them and smiled, before focusing on the water again. For a while no one said a word, each allowing the other to take in the calmness of nature, a blessing hard to come by in Washington DC.

Finally Mercedes spoke, the diamonds in her ears shining like stars. Looking at the water she took a deep breath. "Lil C moved the Trap out of Marjorie. To stay on the safer side."

Carissa frowned. "Why? We stopped using #745. Even moved the Trap to the building over. We're good now." She hadn't touched coke personally since Marjorie. And her frame was thicker and she never felt better.

Mercedes shrugged, feeling slight pain in her arm from being shot. "I know. But he feels after what happened last winter you both shouldn't take any more chances."

Yvette exhaled. "I agree. Things aren't how they use to be in Emerald. Where we knew everyone and they looked out for us. People in Marjorie are looking for a way to come up and if they can make it on us that's exactly what they'll do. Over their bloody bodies of course. We just aren't safe."

Carissa frowned. "We've done more for the Gardens in the short time we ran them than any drug lord before us. And they still have no love for us? Disrespectful ass niggas!"

Yvette shrugged. "They are not our people, Carissa." She paused before looking at Mercedes. "But what I want to know is why Mercedes keeps using the word *you both* lately. What's up with that, friend? You trying to tell us something?"

Mercedes looked at her, walked to the comfortable burgundy lounge chair behind them and sat down. "I'm out the game."

Yvette's jaw dropped and her heart broke.

Instantly.

She'd experienced pain before but for some reason she was taking this the hardest. Never had she dreamed of moving dope in any fashion without Mercedes at her side. "What you mean you out the game? You fucking crazy?"

"I can't do this no more, 'Vette. We have Ryan now and I want to make sure that he comes up in the best way possible. I don't want him being involved in the drug world like Lil C and Chante. Or having to fear for his life all the time. I want him to have a fighting chance and to do that I have to keep him from around it all."

"And how you plan on doing that without money?" Carissa yelled moving closer to her. "I don't know if you realize it but the future you describing can't be done without cold hard cash. College cost money. Living cost money. You better think things through, old friend."

"I've thought it through already. I was going to tell you both before the takedown at Marjorie but we found ourselves at war. And with me shot there was no time. Keep in mind this all happened while Ryan was in the building at that. What would've happened if someone charged our apartment? I can't risk something happening to him."

Yvette was so angry her nostrils flared. "You promised that this life was to the death." She pointed to the ground. "You said that to me when we bought our first pack from Dreyfus. When we took over Emerald City. If I even thought there was a chance that you would not be here I would've never taken it."

Mercedes leapt up and grabbed both of their hands. "Then come with me." She grinned. "We have enough money to walk away from all of this shit and be good forever. Let's be for real, how far can you go in life when your sole purpose is selling drugs? Let's get out while we still can, with our freedom."

Yvette snatched away from her. "Bitch, you sound crazy!"

"Yvette!" Mercedes yelled. "Why you coming at me like that?"

"If you walk away from the dope, you walk away from me," Yvette continued. "So decide. What you wanna do? Live in fake peace with 88, while C still doesn't know? Or us?"

"Wait...so...so you're giving me an ultimatum." Mercedes' lips trembled.

"Me or the world out there, Mercedes!" Yvette yelled pointing at nature. "I'm your sister." She looked at Carissa. "We both are. But if you walk away from the game we will disown you."

Mercedes stared into Carissa's eyes and then Yvette's before a single tear trailed down her face. "I...I...I'm out of the game." She took a deep breath. "I love you both and I'm so sorry. I'll be taking some time with 88 to clear my mind, please don't come looking for me." She stomped away.

Carissa paced the veranda before approaching Yvette. "Are you sure that was the right thing to do? Threatening her? What if we lose her forever?"

PITBULLS IN A SKIRT

Yvette held her stomach and sat down. She felt as if she wanted to throw up. It was then that she realized when she killed Thick and even Heavy it was because in her dreams she'd seen all four of them growing old together.

Her, Mercedes, Kenyetta and Carissa.

Who needed a man when you had sisters?

But now all of that was changed.

"Mercedes, *is* cocaine," Yvette said slowly. "It's in her blood. There's no way she can walk away from the game without feeling the pain of withdrawals. I'm just helping her out that's all. She'll be back."

Mercedes drove down the street in her Bentley on the way to her mansion in Mitchellville, Maryland. Yvette's painful words caused her immediate flu like symptoms but she was sticking by her plan to leave the game once and for all.

It wasn't in her heart anymore.

The thing is Karen and Oscar from the Black Water Klan were trailing behind her with a purpose of their own.

Revenge.

PITBULLS IN A SKIRT

MIKAL MALONE

CARTEL PUBLICATIONS
PRESENTS

The Cartel Publications Order Form

www.thecartelpublications.com
Inmates **ONLY** receive novels for $10.00 per book.
(Mail Order **MUST** come from inmate directly to receive discount)

Shyt List 1	_____	$15.00
Shyt List 2	_____	$15.00
Shyt List 3	_____	$15.00
Shyt List 4	_____	$15.00
Shyt List 5	_____	$15.00
Pitbulls In A Skirt	_____	$15.00
Pitbulls In A Skirt 2	_____	$15.00
Pitbulls In A Skirt 3	_____	$15.00
Pitbulls In A Skirt 4	_____	$15.00
Pitbulls In A Skirt 5	_____	$15.00
Victoria's Secret	_____	$15.00
Poison 1	_____	$15.00
Poison 2	_____	$15.00
Hell Razor Honeys	_____	$15.00
Hell Razor Honeys 2	_____	$15.00
A Hustler's Son	_____	$15.00
A Hustler's Son 2	_____	$15.00
Black and Ugly	_____	$15.00
Black and Ugly As Ever	_____	$15.00
Year Of The Crackmom	_____	$15.00
Deadheads	_____	$15.00
The Face That Launched A	_____	$15.00
Thousand Bullets		
The Unusual Suspects	_____	$15.00
Miss Wayne & The Queens of DC	_____	$15.00
Paid In Blood (eBook Only)	_____	$15.00
Raunchy	_____	$15.00
Raunchy 2	_____	$15.00
Raunchy 3	_____	$15.00
Mad Maxxx	_____	$15.00
Quita's Daycare Center	_____	$15.00
Quita's Daycare Center 2	_____	$15.00
Pretty Kings	_____	$15.00
Pretty Kings 2	_____	$15.00
Pretty Kings 3	_____	$15.00
Silence Of The Nine	_____	$15.00
Silence Of The Nine 2	_____	$15.00
Prison Throne	_____	$15.00
Drunk & Hot Girls	_____	$15.00
Hersband Material	_____	$15.00
The End: How To Write A	_____	$15.00
Bestselling Novel In 30 Days (Non-Fiction Guide)		
Upscale Kittens	_____	$15.00
Wake & Bake Boys	_____	$15.00
Young & Dumb	_____	$15.00
Young & Dumb 2:	_____	$15.00

PITBULLS IN A SKIRT

Tranny 911	_____	$15.00
Tranny 911: Dixie's Rise _____		$15.00
First Comes Love, Then Comes Murder _____		$15.00
Luxury Tax	_____	$15.00
The Lying King	_____	$15.00
Crazy Kind Of Love	_____	$15.00
And They Call Me God	_____	$15.00
The Ungrateful Bastards	_____	$15.00
Lipstick Dom	_____	$15.00
A School of Dolls	_____	$15.00
Hoetic Justice	_____	$15.00
KALI: Raunchy Relived	_____	$15.00
Skeezers	_____	$15.00
You Kissed Me, Now I Own You	_____	$15.00
Nefarious	_____	$15.00
Redbone 3: The Rise of The Fold	_____	$15.00
Clown Niggas	_____	$15.00

(**Redbone 1 & 2** are **NOT** Cartel Publications novels and if **ordered** the cost is **FULL** price of $15.00 **each**. **No Exceptions**.)

Please add $5.00 **PER BOOK** for shipping and handling.

The Cartel Publications * P.O. BOX 486 OWINGS MILLS MD 21117

Name: _____

Address: _____

City/State: _____

Contact/Email: _____

Please allow 5-7 BUSINESS days before shipping.

The Cartel Publications is NOT responsible for Prison Orders rejected.

NO PERSONAL CHECKS ACCEPTED

STAMPS NO LONGER ACCEPTED

CPSIA information can be obtained
at www.ICGtesting.com
Printed in the USA
LVOW12s1535100117
520452LV00002B/301/P